MISSING THE RULES

ALSO BY MARIAH DIETZ

MISSING THE RULES

A DATING PLAYBOOK NOVELLA BOOK: 6.5

MARIAH DIETZ

Cover by: Kate Farlow, Y'all That Graphic

❀ Created with Vellum

MISSING THE RULES

**BOOK 6.5 IN THE DATING PLAYBOOK
SERIES**

This novella takes place prior to the epilogue in Writing the Rules. It is intended to be read after Bending the Rules and Breaking the Rules, but is recommended to be read after finishing all six books in the series. Start reading Bending the Rules Now.

1

RAEGAN

I roll over in protest as the alarm goes off.

Reality is so unappealing this close to Christmas. All I want to do is wear cozy sweatpants, drink my weight in hot cocoa, and watch every Christmas movie on TV. Memories sift through my thoughts, ones of being home at my parents, Gramps and Camilla over, Mom sitting on the couch with a pile of papers, and Dad bringing out the Crockpot filled with little smokies. Paxton would be stretched across the couch, Maggie prodding him, telling him to sit up and reminding him he's taking up too much room. I'd be checking the weather forecast every hour for snow and sitting as close to the tree as possible, high on the scents of pine and Christmas.

A warm arm hooks around my waist, pulling me against an even hotter chest. "What time did you get home last night?" Lincoln's voice is like sandpaper this early in the morning. I love it.

"Late," I say, my voice just above a whisper, eyes still closed.

He releases a quiet sigh before pressing his lips to my shoulder. "Get some sleep. I'll try and call you this afternoon."

I wrack my brain to recall what day of the week it is, my thoughts stopping on Wednesday. The realization has me opening my eyes and twisting to face him. Without warning, I pretzel myself around

his waist and shoulders. Wednesdays are one of their longest practice days of the week, referred to as an "install day" because the
team learns the playbook of their upcoming competitors. It's a long
day filled with drills and workouts, meetings, and classroom time
that will have him gone for the next thirteen hours. Lincoln
chuckles a low and throaty sound as he twists to face me, his hands
going to my thighs, drawing me closer. His heart beats against mine,
steady and strong like a drumbeat. I want to strip my clothes, forget
time and responsibilities, and make his heart and breaths grow
erratic.

"The season's almost over," he says softly while I breathe him in.

I love football, and I love that Lincoln gets to live out his dream.
But there are days I struggle to love how much and how hard he has
to work.

I'm in the second year of my master's program, another thief of all
free time, and finding time together some days feels like a chore.
Even on days when I stay at his condo or when he stays at the apartment I share with Poppy, it feels like we're two ships passing in the
night.

His backup alarm sounds, the one that warns if he doesn't get up
and leave in the next few minutes, he'll be late.

I don't want to let him go, but I do.

"I should be out of class around nine."

He used to promise to stay up, but thirteen-hour days led to unin-
tentionally broken promises that he's since stopped issuing.

He plants a kiss on my mouth, his hands still securing me to him,
then pulls back and stares at me. It's too dark to see the color of his
irises, but I feel the intensity and seriousness in his gaze all the same.
"I'll meet you at seven-thirty. We'll grab something to eat before your
class."

He knows every part of my crazy schedule like it's a second playbook that he's memorized. It's a seemingly small detail, but one that
makes my heart swell. I lean in and kiss him, breathing in his heady
scent, cedar, spice, and something fresh that always reminds me of
the Pacific Ocean that has my thoughts diving into more images of

him naked and on top of me. I inwardly groan as he slips from the bed.

I reach for the bedside lamp and turn it on so I can watch him saunter to the closet naked except for his boxer briefs, where he tugs on a pair of sweatpants. "Forget food. Let's spend the twenty minutes in the backseat of your truck."

Lincoln's gaze snaps to mine, a predatory gleam in his eyes before he crosses the room in two bounds and claims my mouth with his. My entire body reacts to his heat and weight. Need and desire pull me closer. I wrap my arms around his broad shoulders, desperate to feel him everywhere as his lips mark me with promises.

His phone rings from the nightstand, reminding us both that he has to leave. He groans, his fingers brushing against my bare skin under my tee. He kisses me again, this time softly, sweetly, like a roller coaster car after the big drop when the kinetic energy is too great to simply come to a stop and has to coast to the end. My body rejects the slowed pace, disappointment a familiar weight in my chest.

Lincoln swallows, pulling me closer. The beat of his heart is faster, charged, and his desire for me sits like a steel bar between my legs, reminding me he isn't ready to stop either. He rests his forehead against mine. "I'll see you at seven-thirty, Kerosene." He kisses me again, then pulls the sheet and blankets back just enough to slip out, keeping the majority of the warmth still tucked into bed with me as he reaches for his phone.

Lincoln strides back to the closet, his bare torso on full display, chiseled perfection that makes being awake entirely worthwhile. "Hey, Coach," he says, answering his phone while grabbing a clean tee. The Latin verse tattooed across his ribs flashes at me before disappearing beneath white cotton.

He nods at something his coach has said. "Yeah, I'm leaving now." He nods again. "Okay. Yeah. See you in fifteen." He hangs up before swinging his eyes back to me. "You should get some rest."

"Just getting some dream inspiration."

His smile is instant and so wide it demands reciprocation. I love when he smiles at me like this—when life and responsibilities aren't keeping him focused and controlled. He stalks over to the bed and plants his fists on the mattress, leaning his face close to mine. "Two months left, and then I'm going to be waking you up every morning with my head between your legs." He bends and sucks my nipple into his mouth through my T-shirt, causing the ache between my legs to intensify.

He sits up, and I moan my objection, missing the heat of his mouth, before he kisses me again, hard and deep. "I love you," he says, staring down at me.

"I love you."

A low growl rumbles in his throat as he brings his lips to mine once again. "I'll see you tonight. Try and get a little more sleep." His kiss is a whisper as he stands to finally leave.

I roll to my back, trying to shake off the disappointment that swims through my veins with his absence.

He has three games left in the season, and then his schedule will lighten considerably. But this assurance fails to settle me because just three days after his final game of the season, I'll be leaving for six weeks to do a field study in Mexico. It's an opportunity that I've been looking forward to for months, yet as it crawls closer, I'm beginning to dread the trip.

I flip off the light and release a deep breath, rolling until I find Lincoln's pillow and bury my face into the fabric, breathing him in. It's a slight reprieve, but my thoughts are awake, and the list of things I need to accomplish are running through my mind like a catchy and unwanted chorus. I slide on my glasses and flip off the blankets, the cold air stinging my bare legs.

A hot pink sticky note sits on the coffee machine where a half pot of coffee waits for me in the kitchen. Lincoln doesn't drink coffee during the season, but he makes it for me every morning. He likely knew better than me that I wouldn't be able to go back to sleep. I walk closer and read:

"Kick ass today. Love you."

I grab the mug I had gotten last year from my step-grandma, Camilla. It's shaped like a snowman and makes my holiday-loving heart happy, especially since we haven't had time to set up any decorations—another casualty of not having enough time and me living under two roofs.

I fix my coffee and sit down at the kitchen table. When we picked out the dining set, I'd imagined dinner parties with our friends, game nights, and Friendsgiving. It had been in the days following Lincoln being drafted to the Seattle Seahawks, keeping him here in Washington with me while I finished my junior and senior years at Brighton University. We were still celebrating the draft victories of our tightly knit group, naïve to the drastic changes that were about to follow. Within weeks, we were spread across the country. Paxton went to play for the Saints in New Orleans, Ian went to California to play for the Chargers, and Arlo went to New York to play for the Jets. Olivia chose to go with Arlo, making another huge move. Rose stayed in Seattle for a few months, but like Poppy, she quickly discovered how difficult a long-distance relationship was and opted to move to California and open her first yoga studio there. Chloe, Nessie, Tyler, and Cooper were here for another year, which helped ease some of the sting, but the following year, Chloe was accepted to Yale to complete her master's degree, and the other three followed. Thankfully, Pax was traded to the Seahawks the same year, bringing him back home and allowing him to live out his dream of playing for his favorite team.

Seattle is still home base for Olivia, Rose, and Ian, who all have family, drawing them back, but it's less frequent.

I go to grab some yogurt from the fridge, catching sight of the invitation tacked to the front with a magnet from the aquarium—an invitation to Arlo and Olivia's wedding this February. My smile spreads to my heart. I've been looking forward to us all being together since we heard the news of their engagement in June.

I take my yogurt back to the table and open my laptop, working to reel in every ounce of energy and focus I can muster, and get to work on a paper that's due Friday. I've never been a procrastinator, yet it feels like I'm in a constant cycle of procrastination due to the vigorous work and deadlines constantly assigned.

I spend the next three hours buried in the assignment until I have to get ready to go to the aquarium. I only work a few days a week now, my hours cut to make time for my schooling—another sacrifice that I remind myself is necessary to reach my goal of becoming a cetologist.

"Hey, Rae!" Greta Alsman, our chief resident marine biologist, greets me as I hang my coat, a large box of doughnuts in her hands. "Did you hear the music when you walked in?" Her eyes are alight with mischief. Every December, there are arguments over the music played. Greta loves a mixture of Christmas classics, while others prefer instrumental, and some prefer pop. The rule is whoever unlocks the aquarium that day gets to select the music, and Hans has been the early bird for the past week, leading to five straight days of instrumental soundtracks.

I grin to share in her victory and fail to mention that Hans is out today. She'll realize it soon enough.

"Lois emailed me pictures of the baby orcas from Pod L that you guys saw over the weekend." Joy shines from her eyes. Lois Chavis is part of the tribal team researching the Puget Sound, tracking the orcas and other marine life. "You guys got some amazing shots," Greta says.

"That was all Joe," I say, referring to another member of our team as I reach for the giant rubber boots that I wear while here.

"Before you get changed...." Greta visibly winces. "Here, have a doughnut while I ask you for a favor."

I sit back in my seat and look at her, noting her apprehensive smile and groove between her eyes.

"Front desk duty?" I ask. We've recently had a difficult time keeping someone in the role. It's a high attrition position because people are often left alone in the lobby for long periods, fielding questions and angry customers.

Hope sparks in her eyes. "No... But...." She cringes. "You're my only diver today...." Her trailed-off sentence means one thing—I have to dive into our large tank this afternoon to feed the fish and clean the windows. During the years that I volunteered here, I floated between nearly all responsibilities, including preparing food for the animals, assisting our vet, educating guests, and more. Diving, however, requires a special license that I didn't acquire until two years ago, and I rarely use it while here because we have a list of volunteer divers who enjoy the task. Unfortunately, the holidays often leave this to fall upon Anton, and today, me.

I try not to look disappointed by the news. After all, few are lucky enough to love their job, and I genuinely do. However, diving is still something I struggle with after nearly drowning five years ago, and the wolf eels only add to my anxiety. They're not venomous, or dangerous, or even eels for that matter—just bizarre-looking fish—but there's something about their size, the way they move, and their blatant curiosity that sends chills up my spine.

"It's okay. I could use a refresher. I haven't been scuba diving since September, and I'll need to suit up for Mexico."

Greta's smile is hopeful as she shoves the box of doughnuts closer to me.

I shake my head, trying to avoid the look of pity she directs at me. "Maybe I'll race the wolf eels. See if they can catch me."

This has her laughing again because they're notoriously slow swimmers. "I'll help get their food ready."

Once dressed in my drysuit and scuba gear, I drop into the tank, my heart thumping wildly in my chest. The chamber is filled with local plants and fish that move as I swim deeper.

A little girl is on the opposite side of the glass, pointing at me and smiling. I swim lower until I'm even with her and wave. She dances in place, giggling and waving until her mom beckons her forward. I focus on my task and start cleaning the glass from the inside, going over the large window decals of Santa and snowflakes painted on the opposite side of the tank.

While I scrub the glass, fish weave around me, darting close and then swimming away. It doesn't take long for one of the wolf eels to approach me. Divers often enjoy wolf eels in the open waters since they're known for being calm and gentle. Our divers can even tell our wolf eels apart, recognizing them by their unique patterns of dark spots that cover their heads and bodies. A shiver runs up my spine as it swims closer. It's nearly eight feet long and has three lines of molars across its top jaw and two more on the bottom, strong enough to break the shells of sea urchins, clams, and crabs, and most definitely my hand if it chose to. Unlike some of the other fish that seem to forget this daily process, the wolf eels know that a diver's presence means food, and it circles me, searching for the food that is still being prepared.

On the other side of the glass, more families gather, and another employee at the aquarium stands in the corner, a mic in hand. Without hearing her, I know that she's introducing me and the numerous fishes, specifically the wolf eels, which often garner a lot of attention during feedings.

I finish cleaning the window, then proceed to feed the fish, an activity that garners an even larger audience. One of the wolf eels puts his mouth on my arm twice but doesn't bite, reminding me my fears are mostly in my head like they are about most things regarding diving, deep water, and the chances I'll get caught on something while I'm underwater.

2

LINCOLN

"**D**amn," Pax remarks as I pour sand from my shoes. I clap the soles together to get the stray grains out and then peel off my socks. Wednesdays are one of the three days a week I work on strength training and speed, my routine grueling and explosive. Working out in college was to ensure we remained strong and in shape, but since being drafted, it's a whole new ballgame. I'm no longer working to be better than those graduating high school, most of whom hadn't filled out or gained their full potential. In the NFL, I'm competing against the biggest, strongest, and fastest—the absolute best football players in the world.

Pax takes a seat next to me. He's been struggling with his own bag of issues, ones that revolve around the fact he went from being one of the best-known players in college, starting every game and loved by spectators to not seeing a single minute of a game, waiting for the current quarterback, Brevard, to retire at the end of this season. I roll my shoulder and stretch my neck.

"Are you ready for the team meeting?" Pax asks.

"This week is going to be a bitch," I say in response. We're playing against our rivals, the Forty-Niners, which has everyone on overdrive, determined to win.

Paxton leans back. "I don't know how players transition to coaching. These past couple of years have been hell."

"I overheard Brevard talking about the property he and his wife are buying in Maine. I think everything's still a go for him to retire at the end of the season."

"I feel like a fuckwad for hoping he does." He hastily swipes through his light brown hair, sweat making it stick up in all directions. No doubt feeling conflicted because Brevard has been one hell of a leader for the team and will leave massive shoes to fill.

"You shouldn't," I tell him, shaking my head. Paxton has to work just as hard as every other player on the team and come to every damn practice but doesn't get to see the field. I'd be going out of my mind. Rae, however, claims these years have been a benefit to Pax, certain that he's learning to read the team and how to execute on strengths and diminish weaknesses, and if there's anyone I trust about football and understanding the nuances, it's her.

Pax releases a breath and stretches as he gets to his feet. "This should be your week, though," he says, proving Rae's point. "They're slow and won't be able to keep up with you. You'll need to watch the corner, but this might be the game you actually make a fan or two." He grins like he's proud of his insult.

Fans have never been what pushes me. The noise of the crowd can be intoxicating when the team goes on a run, but I don't give a single shit if people recognize or know me. Unfortunately, my nickname as the President followed me to the NFL, and the press loves using the moniker when referring to me.

I follow him down the maze of halls toward our team meeting. "Is Rae flying to California?" he asks.

I shake my head. "She wanted to, but she's been buried with school. I've barely seen her lately."

Pax frowns. "She's never known how to slow down." Her dual degrees in biology and zoology attest to his point.

"Maggie will be here on Monday," Paxton reminds me of their older sister, flying in from where she currently resides in Guatemala. The trio is inseparable, which offers me a gutter of relief because I know Rae's been struggling with balancing school and her social life. Maggie will refuse to be ignored, something my schedule makes nearly impossible.

"That's good," I say.

Pax glances at me as we pass through the door into one of the conference rooms where the team is beginning to gather and nods knowingly.

Tablets are passed around the room, filled with details and plays of the Forty-Niners, notes about where we'll need to execute and consider.

The meeting bleeds into another until dinner is ready. We eat most of our meals here at the practice facility, where a team of nutritionists determines our calories, protein, and carbs. Coach requests that we eat together for more than just the strict nutritional aspects, believing this time helps us build and strengthen our bond as a team which is visible and vital on the field.

By the time we leave, it's already seven-thirty. I call Rae as I put my truck into gear.

"Hey," she answers.

"I'm sorry, babe. I'm late," I tell her, punching the gas. "I'm on my way."

"It's okay," she says, but I hear the disappointment in her voice. "By the time you get here, I'll only have two minutes before I have to leave for class. You should head home and relax. Ice your shoulder and fold my clothes that I left in the dryer."

I grin. "I'll take your two minutes over nothing."

"I'm in the opposite direction of your condo."

"I remember where campus is." I don't mention that I'd fucking walk if I had to.

She's silent for a second. "If you come to the upper lot, I can probably give you five minutes."

"Sold."

When I pull into the lot, she's standing on the sidewalk with her coat zipped up to her chin. I unlock the doors as she walks to the passenger side. Her blonde hair is pulled back, exposing her red cheeks. She smiles as she opens the door and climbs in.

"You look cold," I say, leaning close to meet her for a kiss.

"I hope it snows." She always does, but in Seattle, we rarely get snow, and when we do, it's generally in January and only a dusting.

"Maybe next year we can rent a cabin for Christmas, somewhere where they have tons of snow."

Her blue eyes shine with possibilities. "I don't know. We might have to wait until you retire for that."

I lean in, sealing my lips over hers as images of what our lives will look like in a decade fill my head, holding onto the casual assuredness that we'll be together. She reaches for me, running her fingers through my hair. She tastes like chocolate, cinnamon, and addiction.

Her eyes are still closed, a wistful smile on her lips as she sits back and lifts her fingers in front of the vents blowing warm air. "How was practice?"

The last thing I want to do is talk about practice. "What time are you going to be home?"

"I have a study group, so probably not until eleven."

"Wake me up."

"You have to be up at five, again."

I thread my fingers into her hair, my palm resting against her jaw. "I'll fold your laundry, then go to bed. That way, when you wake me up at eleven, I'll still have my full eight hours of sleep."

A laugh breaks through her before she licks her lips. Hints of lust dance in her eyes as she stares at me. "Clothing better be optional when I wake you up."

"They're against all the fucking rules."

Her smile grows.

I lean forward, kissing her again as time fights against me. My lips linger on hers, not daring to go as far as we had this morning. "Come on. I'll walk you to class." I turn off the engine and open my door before she can protest and tell me someone might recognize me.

The sky is clear tonight, making it several degrees colder. We close our doors in unison, meeting on the sidewalk. I wrap an arm around her shoulders, tucking her against me. Suggestions of her calling in sick or crawling into the cab of my truck and forgetting about where either of us needs to be form in my head and cloud my thoughts.

"Maybe I should go to California with you this weekend? I could probably get the class notes online."

My gaze drops to hers. "Will you be drowning in homework?"

"I can get some of it done on the plane. I can pack after we go to dinner with your dad on Friday."

"Shit. I forgot about Friday." I drop my head back a few degrees. My relationship with my dad has improved over the past few years. However, I still can't stand my stepmom, Carol, and recently, my dad's been flakey as all hell which usually means business is taking his top priorities. He disappears for long periods before reappearing and acts like not hearing from him in months is normal and acceptable. It is now that I'm an adult—it wasn't when I was a kid.

"We can make it short," Rae says. "I can tell him I have a ton of homework, and it won't even be a lie."

I pull her tighter. This game is one of the most important of the year because they're our rivals and having Rae in the crowd is one of the few factors that seem to impact my game because knowing she's watching me makes me play smarter, better. However, asking her to be there seems selfish when her own plate is so full. "You should stay and catch up with school and sleep and be my consolation prize in case we lose."

Her smile that I love so much, breaks when I stare at her. "I'm going to be leaving soon. I feel like we should be stealing as much time as we possibly can right now."

"Remind me never to introduce you to any more marine biologists," I say before kissing the crown of her head.

She smiles, but her eyes are downcast, and her lips dip too quickly.

"Hey, hey." I come to a stop, shifting, so we're face to face. "I'm kidding. We've got this. Six weeks will go by in a flash." I'm trying to convince myself as much as I am her. "We're seasoned pros."

Amateurs, actually, but Rae went on her first trip to study conservation the summer of her freshman year and has gone twice more since, and it's always to remote areas where she barely has reception, and I spend six weeks losing my mind.

Rae takes a breath through her nose, eyes locked on mine. Then, slowly, she nods. "You're right."

"And then we'll be heading to Vegas for the bachelor and bachelorette parties, and then we have two weeks before heading to New Jersey."

Her lips curl, and her gaze softens as if an invisible weight is lifted from her shoulders. "You're right again."

We walk the remainder of the distance, hands locked together. While we were both at Brighton, we still had to work for these moments, but not nearly as damn hard as we do now.

We stop outside the door, and Rae turns to me, fingers still twined with mine. "I'll see you at eleven?"

I lean close, my lips grazing her ear. "I'm going to make you forget your name tonight."

3

RAEGAN

On my way to study group, I return the texts I've been meaning to reply to for the past couple of days. Poppy, touching base and asking if I want to go Christmas shopping next week. Mom, asking how I'm feeling and a second message telling me how proud she is. Gramps, reminding me that Camilla is on a baking spree and would like opinions on her new cookies, asking me to give him a window when they can drop them off.

Guilt hits with each message and quick response that I issue. Christmas is next week. I only have four more days of classes, and then I intend to spend the five days of break packing in as much quality time as I can.

I slip my phone back into my bag and take a seat next to Mila Morales. Mila has become my closest friend here at school. We share a love for all things that involve coffee, Dr. Pepper, books, and marine biology. She places a coffee in front of me, the hot steam smelling both sweet and dark.

"You're a lifesaver."

She smiles. "We made it to hump day," she says, reaching for her own cup. "Two more days until the weekend."

I take out my laptop, thinking about California and how much fun it would be. Poppy is going to the game too, and Ian and Rose are going because it's a bye week for Ian. It would be so much fun but admittedly difficult, setting me back and making preparing for the break even more stressful. As conversations begin, I reach for my coffee, all thoughts of trips set aside for the next few hours.

THE KITCHEN LIGHT is on when I step through the front door of Lincoln's condo.

I set my bag on one of the dining room chairs and take a brief look around. The lease for the house that Lincoln, Caleb, Arlo, and Paxton rented together through college ended just a month after they graduated, a contingency in case they weren't drafted. The draft occurred at the end of April, and Lincoln was a first draft pick, ensuring he wouldn't get cut at the end of preseason, but he stayed in the house until the lease ended.

When Lincoln started house shopping, he did it a bit like most things he doesn't like: growly and reluctant, revealing that moving out and closing that chapter of his life was a bitter aftertaste to his dreams coming true.

The relator had three selections, and this was the smallest and farthest from the stadium, but it was the closest to the aquarium.

I slide off my shoes and quietly pad to the master bedroom and open the door. The lights are off, and Lincoln's on his side, fast asleep. He used to be a light sleeper, waking up whenever I got home, but over time, he's become accustomed to my random hours, now sleeping through my late nights most of the time.

I'm cold and tired, overwhelmed and hungry, and thoughts of Christmas and travel are on the fringes of my thoughts, threatening to keep me up for hours. One look at Lincoln and seeing how exhausted he is, adds a shade of guilt to my emotions. I consider letting him sleep and changing his alarm to go off an hour earlier and spending time with him then, but before I can calculate what time I'll need to set the alarm for, Lincoln rolls to his back and blinks.

"What time is it?" he asks.

"Just after eleven." I edge closer to the bed. "You look exhausted. You should sleep."

He tags me around the wrist. "I took a nap, remember?" His fingers slide down to mine. I rotate my wrist, so our palms are flush, his hot and calloused against my constantly cold skin.

Lincoln pulls the blankets back and stands. "How was class?" His voice is soft and smooth like leather as he leans close, his lips connecting with my neck.

"Long." My answer is vague and honest. As much as I love learning, earning my master's degree hasn't been quite what I'd expected. I've read more in the past year than my entire academic career, and I constantly feel like I'm in a state of information overload, trying to remember facts and data that are listed off in lectures like common adverbs.

He chuckles, his tongue tracing the skin behind my ear. "So many inappropriate innuendos." His teeth graze my skin, sending a bolt of heat and desire through me so fast I forget what he just said. "How was your study group."

"I don't want to talk about my study group," I say, turning into him, so our chests meet.

He kisses along my jaw as he settles his hands on my waist. "What do you want to talk about?"

The only thing I want him to tell me right now is that he's been thinking about me all day, wanting me in the same desperate ways I want him. I want his voice to turn gravelly like it does when he's turned on and tell me all the dirty and wonderful things he wants to do to me. "Less talking. More kissing."

I feel his smile against my jaw and the soft rumble of his laugh against my chest, but he obliges, his lips colliding with mine like we're puzzle pieces that were crafted to seal together. My breath is a moan as I lean into him, the faint scents of soap and his skin consuming me.

Lincoln gathers the hem of my shirt, drawing it higher, his knuckles skimming over my exposed stomach. He pulls back long enough to free my sweater, and then his mouth is back on mine, breathing life into me.

One of my favorite things about sex with Lincoln is the variety. Hot, fast sex in the shower, my palms pressed against the wall. The desperate, uncontrolled kind that has us hiding away in a friend's bathroom, or the backseat of his truck, or up against the kitchen counter. The slow and sexy times that involve him fingering me while I'm getting ready to go to class or work and me returning the favor as he's trying to have a phone call with his manager, and we're both strung so tight that by the time we finally reach our climax it feels all-consuming. Tonight, I can tell by the assuredness of his actions and control in his kiss that he plans to drag this out and keep his promise to make me forget my name. My stomach curls with desire that has me leaning more fully into him.

He burns trails across my bare skin with his fingers, building my anticipation each time he inches closer to the clasp at the back of my bra, leaving me to kiss him more urgently when he moves his hands away.

At one time, it made me nervous to talk about what I wanted or what felt good sexually, but my confidence has grown over the past several years for a multitude of reasons that largely have nothing to do with sex. It's in the way Lincoln has encouraged and supported my dreams of becoming a cetologist, how he listens with rapt attention to me whenever I talk, and being present emotionally and physically through so many life changes, good decisions, and bad ones. My friends helped strengthen my confidence as well—Poppy is still my ride or die, and she is there through thick and thin, but Rose, Olivia, Chloe, and Vanessa have become huge parts of my life. And my team at the aquarium has been instrumental in their patience and strength in helping me get over my lasting fears of drowning.

"Lincoln," I growl when his hands avert from where I want them.

He grins, his brown eyes are inky with desire and lust. "Yeah, babe."

I reach behind my shoulders and unfasten my bra, dropping it to his bedroom floor.

He covers my breasts with his hands, stroking over the sensitive skin as his lips claim mine. The feeling of his abs against mine, the pressure of his knuckles gently massaging either side of my nipples, and his mouth hot and consuming, has me aching to feel him everywhere. I move my hand over each carefully sculpted ab until my palm connects with his hardened length. His hips shift forward, just as eager for my touch.

Lincoln grips my hips, turning me so that my back faces the bed, and lays me back, his fingers releasing the button on my jeans before hooking into my pants and underwear and shimmying them down my legs. His mouth is on me with my next breath, wasting no time. I gasp and then shudder as pleasure blooms in my body. He knows my body better than he does Ancient Roman history—which is saying something because Lincoln is as brilliant as he is gorgeous. His tongue goes from gentle and exploring to demanding and flat against my most sensitive parts, possessive and claiming over me. My breaths fall faster, their cadence becoming erratic. My mind is consumed with thoughts of pleasure. I fist the bedding and tip my head back, and right when I think I'm nearing my tipping point, and my thighs start to tremble, he dips two fingers inside me and synchronizes his movements to draw out an orgasm that leaves me breathless and limp.

Lincoln kisses a trail that begins at my sensitive center and goes up and over my stomach, then across both breasts, dotting my chin, and finally makes his way to my mouth. He pulls the sheet and blanket over me, and I shake my head, finally opening my eyes. Lincoln lies on his side, dark eyes drinking me in like I'm one of the fine pieces of art in his father's personal collection. "You're exhausted," he says. "You should get some sleep."

"I still remember my name," I tell him, reminding him of his earlier threat.

His smile is wide and boastful as he absently follows the scar from my accident with his fingers. "I'm pretty sure you forgot how to even breathe for a second there."

"Sleep is the very last thing I want." I reach between us, palming his hardened length. Lincoln's breath comes out as a hiss that leaves me smiling. I shift to my knees, perpendicular to his hips, and move my hand over him again before adding my tongue. He still has too much focus because he weaves a finger between my legs and gently begins fingering me again, drawing my wetness out and between my folds. My movements become faster, caught in a haze of delicious pleasure as I grind against his hand and stifle my moans on his cock.

I'm chasing my second orgasm when Lincoln moves, smooth and fast like a panther, flipping our positions, so I'm on my back again, and he's hovering over me. His dark eyes connect with mine, a thousand unspoken words spilling into my consciousness. He watches me as he sinks inside me, deliciously slow so that I feel every inch of him. I wait for him to move, desperate for the friction as desire swells like a tsunami, making a list of demands, but Lincoln remains still, gazing at me with that fervent look that makes me feel like a goddess.

I touch his face, trailing my fingers over his cheek, to the hard plane of his jaw, and then over one broad shoulder, the one that he injured years ago and still flares up. "I've missed you," I admit.

He dips, kissing me sweetly, before his hips contradict the gesture, slamming into me, and it feels incredible. "I've missed you," he says, voice uneven as he moves into me again. "But I'll always be back. I'll always be here for you."

I want to ask him to swear on it, but his hips roll forward, the movement so satisfyingly good, I start to nod—yes to him being here, yes to him doing that movement again, and yes to now.

Football has trained him for endurance, a benefit that I certainly reap the benefits of as he moves, finding my second release before his own.

4

LINCOLN

Thursday and Friday are near replicas of Wednesday when it comes to practice: I wake up early, leaving Rae asleep in bed, head to the team facility where my day starts with breakfast, meetings, and training, practice, more meetings, more practice, followed by even more meetings. The information about our opponent's plays is drilled into us, essential so that we can still execute when we're out on the field, clinging to muscle memory when fatigue sets in. On the flip side, it's also vital for us to be prepared to be vultures and pick the hell out of their every last weakness.

I glance at my cellphone. It's Friday evening. I was supposed to leave here thirty minutes ago to pick up Rae so we could meet my dad and stepmom for dinner. Instead, I sent her a text twenty minutes ago with an apology asking her to meet me there. Our season has been riddled with losses, a new acceptance that I'm looking forward to testing next year with Paxton on the field with me.

The team is counting on me this week, with a game where I'm our best chance at breaking the Forty-Niner's defense. Brevard, our current quarterback, has one hell of an arm, but he collapses too fast, and fear is apparent if the defenders get within three feet of him.

Those occasions blind him to the field and where everyone is, and lead to a panicked Hail Mary pass that is always short, thus making my job twice as hard.

Coach taps his fist against the tabletop. "All right, we'll see you guys tomorrow. Be sure to drink, rest, and make sure we're all preparing mentally for this game."

We file out, guilt stretching my gait because I'm late twice in one week, both times at Rae's expense.

"President," one of my teammates calls, but I wave him off, making it to my car, where I call Rae and start the engine.

"Hey," she answers on the third ring, her voice a strange contradiction of chipper and nervous.

"I'm sorry, babe. I'm on my way now. Is my dad there?"

"Yup. We just ordered some appetizers."

"Shit. I'm sorry." I press the gas pedal to go faster.

"It's okay," she says. "We're just catching up."

"Is he trying to give you a guilt trip?" I ask, trying to guess at the tension in her voice.

"I've got a *lot* of homework," she says, reminding me of her making this excuse so we could get out of dinner early.

"It's that bad?"

"Yup."

"Shit. I'm sorry, babe. I'm on my way."

"No. You should take your time. Drive safely."

I inwardly groan, wondering if he's delivering one of his epic speeches about me not living up to my potential or expectations. "I'm sorry," I say again. "I love you."

"I love you, too," she says. "Don't rush."

I glance at my speedometer and ease my foot off the gas. Coach would have my balls if I were to make the news for speeding.

Traffic is busy, Friday nights in Seattle always are, and my dad insisted we go to dinner at Prospector's Grill, his favorite steak restaurant located smack dab in the center of the city. Shoppers are everywhere, scrambling to get last-minute gifts. Christmas lights adorn every storefront and lamppost. I know if Rae were in the passenger seat, she'd be pointing out all the penguins she sees because they're her favorite.

I grab the sport coat I'd dropped in my backseat for this very purpose and tug it on. I used to find these dinners stifling and contrived—filled with guilt trips and barely masqueraded fearmongering to make me follow in my father's and work at the law firm he's now a partner at. But, over the past few years, things have improved between us. I still don't call him to hang out and have a beer, but a reconciliation process has begun. He no longer talks about my playing football like it's my greatest mistake, and he knows I don't give a single shit about impressing his friends or clients or anyone else for that matter, with the exception of those I care about. That list of people is short, but I'd move entire mountains for them. And for the first time since he and my mom divorced, he's been married to the same woman for five years, a record for him.

The valet attendant takes my keys in exchange for a small blue ticket that I tuck into my pocket, and then I head through the open doors of the steakhouse.

The inside of the restaurant is like stepping inside of a cave, all dark woods, no windows, lit only by sconces that hang on the walls every few feet, and low overhead lighting. The tables are too close together, and gold curtains hang from floor to ceiling near the doorways. It's looked the same my entire life.

The hostess greets me, eyes bright with recognition. She doesn't ask the question I can see burning in her irises, for which I'm grateful. She likely can't. "I'm here to meet my party, Beckett. Party of four."

She smiles and tries to discreetly elbow another hostess beside her who's helping another customer as she gathers a menu. "Right this way, sir."

She leads me through the maze of compactly arranged tables. I notice Rae first. Her blonde hair is down and curled, a black dress hugging her shoulders and torso. She turns in her seat, as though feeling my stare, and her blue eyes flare with panic as she moves her chair back and stands, smile brittle, hands wringing, distracting me from taking in the sight of the rest of her dress.

Guilt has me wishing the hostess would hurry. Things might be improving with my dad, but he's still an asshole by trade and has likely been giving Raegan advice that includes her quitting school and work because though he'll never admit he's a chauvinist, he's the damn definition.

My attention turns from her to my dad, ready to nail him with a look of warning because we've talked at great lengths about Rae's career ambitions and how he's not allowed to meddle. My attention, however, is snagged on an occupied highchair sitting at the end of the table and then by the blonde woman sitting next to my dad, who is most definitely not my stepmom, Carol.

Rae purses her lips, her forehead marred with regret and sympathy that still isn't registering. I glance toward Dad, waiting for more clues. He leans back in his seat. His hair, which would be fully silver if he didn't still dye it dark to match his younger version and my own dark hair, is combed to one side, his chin held high, defiance shining in his eyes. Warning bells are blowing so damn loud that I don't hear what my dad says as the hostess stops in front of the table. I don't feel anything until Rae wraps her hand around mine and gently squeezes. It's a silent assurance to remind me that she's here and supporting me and a bunch of other encouraging bullshit that normally means the world to me but currently feels dulled as my dad stares me head-on, a silent threat in his dark blue eyes.

"Lincoln," he says. "How was practice? Traffic still busy?"

Rae squeezes my hand even tighter. "We need code words," she whispers, rubbing a hand across her brow to hide her words.

"Where's Carol?" I ask.

Dad turns his head to one side, a warning to my question. "I want you to meet my dear friend Tara." He places a hand on the blonde woman's shoulders.

A server arrives with platters of appetizers, and Rae's the only one who greets and thanks him.

"And your baby brother, Maverick."

I sputter in shock and then cough. "I'm sorry ... my what?"

"You have a little brother," Dad says, turning to look at the little boy.

My eyes swing to the child, blonde, blue-eyed, round cheeks—we look nothing alike. I want to call bullshit, but I know he likely already ordered a paternity test—hell, probably two—and he wouldn't admit this if it weren't true.

"What?" is as articulate as my response comes out, though inside, a war of questions has begun, the first complete one being, "How old is he?"

Rae reaches to grab her silverware in time to keep the child in question from taking them, laughing, and showing off his full set of teeth. He has teeth. He's not a baby. Babies don't have teeth ... right? I have no idea how old children are when they get teeth. I know nothing about babies or kids.

"He just turned two," Dad says.

"Two?" My voice rises.

"Lincoln, sit down." He rubs his brow like he's exhausted by my reaction.

Rae places her hand on mine again, slowing my heart and anger, which is coursing through me like a drug, interfering with my senses.

I slump into my chair, my thoughts working to reassure me that this doesn't matter—his choices don't define me. *Astra indlinant, sed non obligant*, the stars incline us, they do not bind us. I tattooed these words on my body so I'd remember that whenever my dad or my mom or anyone else in my life—myself included—fucked up, it didn't mean a sealed fate. He had a kid—another failed marriage in a long list of failed marriages.

This doesn't define me.

This doesn't bind me.

Fuck me.

I reach for my water and take a healthy gulp.

"When? How? Where?" I list off the questions.

"Tara and I met a few years ago," he says.

Years.

The word echoes in my cavernous mind, which currently feels

empty as I once again attempt to piece this situation together. I look at the child again. Babies take time. They don't just appear. Months? A year? God, how long is a woman pregnant? I swing my attention to Rae, feeling worse again that I don't know. I should know this shit.

She places her hand atop mine again. "Maybe we should go. This...." She closes her eyes and raises her eyebrows like she's searching for the correct word or term to use. "This was a lot. A ... lot lot." She looks at my dad. "Maybe we should meet again in a few weeks and do this somewhere less public."

"He chose this place on purpose," I say. "His attempt to avoid a scene." I raise my glass. "Right, Dad?"

Across from me, my dad releases a measured breath. He has his lawyer face on, a diplomatic expression that is equal parts friendly, conniving, and condescending. "Lincoln, you're acting like a child. Your brother has more manners than you."

My fingers go to the space between my eyes, hearing the word brother replay again.

"You were married," I say. "Two years ago, you were married."

Indignation has him squaring his shoulders. "We tried to make it work. We tried for years."

A scoff escapes my lips, loud and belligerent. "Bullshit. You weren't even married for three years before you had an affair. How was that trying?"

"This coming from you who's been dating the same girl for those same years and hasn't proposed or even made the decision to move in together?"

Lava is flowing through my veins. Only it's not lava—it's worse, more intense, and far less forgiving. It's anger, pure, undiluted anger. "Raegan is off-limits. Don't you fucking forget it."

He has the good sense to look ashamed, his gaze shifting to Rae at my side and offering an apology before returning to me. "This wasn't how I wanted the evening to go. I knew this would come as a shock to you, but I didn't think you'd be this upset. Otherwise, I would have had this conversation with you at home or one on one.

"My marriage with Carol didn't work. You told me it wouldn't. You prophesized as much at my wedding to her, don't you remember?" He looks at me but doesn't give me the chance to respond. "Tara is loving and caring, and she's given me a second chance to be a father. You know first-hand what a terrible father I was. I worked too much, I was gone all the time, and I was always pushing you. With Maverick, I have a chance to be different—better. I wanted to tell you, but you've been so busy that dates weren't working out, and I figured this might be my only chance unless I wait another few months."

I run my hands through my hair, anger still present, but with it is a myriad of feelings and emotions that have me feeling wrong and cruel, selfish, and so many other damn things that it's overwhelming. The only times I can recall feeling so damn overwhelmed is when I first began developing feelings for Raegan and then again when she nearly drowned.

I steal another look at the toddler, pounding away on an iPad.

There are gaps in my father's story, ones that leave fresh paths of betrayal through my emotions because while it's been a few months since I've seen him, it hasn't been years.

"Good luck with your new family." I stand, and Raegan follows, grabbing her purse.

"Lincoln," Dad says. "Lincoln," he says again when I shove my chair to grant Rae a clear path since we're too close to another table, realizing for the first time how many are staring at us. I ignore him and continue forward.

We make our way to the door where I turn, looking both ways for my truck before recalling the valet took it. I fish the ticket from my pocket and hand it to the man behind the podium, and Rae does the same.

"Shit. I forgot you drove."

"Do you want to ride together?" she asks. "We can come and get your truck tomorrow."

"I won't have time. They don't open until four, and I fly out at eleven."

"I can have someone else help me. My mom or Gramps."

I shake my head. "It's fine. I'll meet you back at the condo."

Reluctance shines in her eyes as they dance across my face, likely trying to gauge how far off the deep end I've fallen.

I place my hands on either side of her face and lower my mouth to hers. "I'm sorry this was our first date in a month, and it turned out to be a fucking circus."

She shakes her head, my hands still holding her. "I'm sorry this happened. I didn't know what to do. I thought about telling you to cancel or not come, but I also thought you should know, and...." She shakes her head, and before she can pick up her litany of apologies again, I kiss her.

"It's not your fault, Rae. None of this was you. It was all him." I pull in a deep breath, filled with the scents of her perfume, her shampoo—her, and it does something to settle my nerves.

Rae's car arrives first, and I follow to where the valet opens her door. I pull out my wallet and hand him a tip before taking his place and holding open the door.

"Are you sure you don't want to ride with me?" she asks.

I shake my head. "I need a few minutes to clear my head. I'll see you at the condo."

She kisses me a final time and gets into her car.

My truck arrives a few minutes later.

I think of my tattoo again, of how long I avoided relationships, afraid I'd be just like my dad. On the ride home, my thoughts pander to my fears, continuously guessing at how I'll fuck up my future. Dread mingles around my career and how many times I've reacted without a thought toward a possible injury or a failed future, and then to Raegan, who is without a doubt my greatest achievement and the one thing I cannot lose.

I pull into my parking spot and turn off the engine. Before I can open my door, Rae does it for me. I cut my attention to her, finally taking her in. The dress is nearly see-through over her arms and the top of her chest and then turns solid black, hugging her down to her knees. The sight of her makes it difficult to breathe, and I curse at my dad again for having distracted me from missing the effect of her earlier.

"You look gorgeous," I tell her, climbing out of my truck.

She smiles shyly. "I got this dress last year, and I've been trying to think of where I could wear it, and now I'm kind of disappointed by my decision. Maybe we should burn it?"

I shake my head. "Not a chance." I wrap an arm around her waist, my hand spanning across the soft curve of her backside.

Rae molds to me, like she knows she alone is the answer to my distress. She kisses me, her lips gentle and plying, before she leans back and looks at me. "Come on. Let's go up to the condo." She reads my emotions like she's so adept at doing. Sometimes it's a terrifying reality that she knows me so well, but most of the time, it's assuring and comforting like now.

"I'm so fucking pissed at him. How long has he known?" I shake my head and drop my hold on her. "Has he known the entire fucking time? Keeping this a secret? What kind of bullshit is he trying to pull?"

"Maybe he didn't know?" Rae says. "I mean, it seems unlikely that he would have kept this a secret for so long."

Annoyance churns in my head, all of it directed at my dad. I grit my teeth and look at Rae, who still manages to see the good in most. "He's adept at having multiple relationships," I tell her. "He's done it more than once." Because my father's terrified of being alone, it's his insurance that he'll have someone there when he finally chooses between two women.

Rae blanches, then frowns, likely thinking of her own dad.

"Fuck him," I say.

She stares at me, then slowly nods.

"Rae?"

She pulls in a breath, her thoughts slipping from being present here with me. "Yeah?"

"Will you marry me?"

5

RAEGAN

I stare at Lincoln, shock and bewilderment having stolen my breath, reminding me of that night years ago when the ocean had done the same. My heart beats hard and frantic in my chest, and my lungs begin to burn.

"No," I say, shaking my head. "Not like this. Not when you're mad at your dad and trying to prove a point." I shake my head again, trying not to be offended when I know Lincoln's hurting from his own demons.

His dark eyes narrow with anger, a reaction I should have expected, because as far as he's come with being open and honest with me, that mask of indifference is always in his hand, ready to be worn when he's feeling vulnerable or hurt. "I'm asking you because I love you. Because we're already committed in every other way," he says, defying the mask. He stares at me, eyebrows locked, giving him an unfair advantage. Lincoln can read my thoughts like he's directing them himself, while currently, I'm reeling.

My heart is beating too hard, shattering and reforming in equal measures as his question and the moment replays in my head. "Can we push pause?"

His eyebrows soar up his forehead, like my response is the last thing he was expecting.

"I love you, but I don't want this to be the moment that defines our future. I don't need candy and flowers and hearts, but...." I shake my head, letting my words trail off while trying to understand the splintering feeling in my chest. "This isn't the story I want to tell our kids one day."

He shakes his head, refusing to look at me. "I need to get some air. Clear my head."

I nod, though I want to object.

He turns toward his truck, climbing in and closing the door without looking back. I move, standing next to my car so I'm out of the way. My entire body feels numb and cold as I detach from the situation and watch the evening play out again in my thoughts. When I'd learned about my father's affair, it had shaken me violently. I can't imagine learning about the situation with such a casual and blasé approach, like Lincoln's father offered, and with a sibling as a lasting product.

Lincoln drives out of sight toward the entrance of the garage. I stare at my car, my instincts slowly kicking in. Reason tells me I shouldn't feel hurt and offended, but no matter how hard I try to shake those feelings, they continue to sneak into my thoughts, wetting my eyes. I've dreamed of getting engaged to Lincoln before knowing him well enough to warrant the fantasy, back when my crush was instinct and allure. I've considered it over the past five years of us dating, imagining what this moment would look like. While I never held expectations, I envisioned declarations of love and affection, a heartfelt and simple moment with the two of us, or possibly surrounded by our friends and family. This felt like a cruel joke in comparison.

I swipe away an errant tear and try to focus on finding my keys.

The drive to the apartment Poppy and I have shared for the past four and a half years is only twenty minutes away but seems like hours tonight.

I head up the two flights of stairs, wishing I'd brought a jacket with me. The small wrap around my arms and shoulders was intended for going from garage to garage. I'm shivering by the time I insert my key into the lock, but it's not a welcomed distraction from the chaos happening in my thoughts and chest.

The heat of the apartment greets me, along with the warm glow of the Christmas lights decorating our tree, and a concerned look from Poppy, who turns as I step inside. "What's going on?" she asks, unfolding herself from the couch where she was writing in her journal, and crossing the space to me.

I shake my head to rebuff her words, but my throat is too tight to speak.

"Rae," she says, her voice filled with sympathy and compassion, her brows knit with unspoken questions.

A tear falls down my cheek, and I shake my head, unable to answer.

Poppy wraps her arms around me, pulling me tight for a hug. Sometimes when I'm not feeling well or having a bad day, I yearn for my mom and my life when I lived at home. Other times, I still yearn for my dad and his terrible jokes and delicious fried chicken and love for academia when I'm trying to chart out my life. But Poppy still feels like family, our twenty-plus-year friendship taking us through so many ups and downs, and experiences that when one of us cries, laughs, scares, or is upset, so is the other one. The familiarity and comfort of her presence unleashes the tears I've been working to keep at bay. Tears of frustration and hurt feelings, and countless emotions I have no explanation for.

Poppy allows me to cry, rubbing a hand soothingly over my shoulders while guiding me to the couch where we sit beside each other, knees, hips, and shoulders pinned together. She moves a tissue box in front of me, one hand still on my back.

"What happened?" she asks when I finally release a long and heavy breath.

"Lincoln's dad is the worst," I admit. "We went to dinner with him tonight, and I thought it was going to be this simple catch-up that would only be slightly rocky if the law firm was mentioned or my leaving for Mexico, but it was a train wreck. An absolute train wreck." I proceed to tell Poppy about the night, about how I'd arrived first and how Lincoln's dad casually introduced me to his girlfriend and son, and how my initial reaction had been to laugh because I genuinely thought he was joking. How my response had created transgression that I was still trying to process when Lincoln arrived, and the shit-show really started.

Poppy stares at me wide-eyed, shaking her head slowly. "Did Lincoln flip out?"

"Yes, not table-flipping level, but enough that it offended his dad, who went into defense mode and insinuated that Lincoln and I aren't serious because we haven't moved in together or gotten engaged."

Poppy's eyes round like saucers. "Tell me this was when Lincoln punched him."

I shake my head, sarcasm and my anger for his dad acting as a tourniquet to my sadness. "No, instead, we went back to Lincoln's condo, and he asked me to marry him."

Poppy jerks her head back, blinking too quickly as she brings a hand up to cover her mouth. "What did you say?"

I shake my head, tears diluting my vision. "I said no."

Poppy's eyes are still round like an owl. "Sorry to make you relive this, but you're killing me a little here. What happened after that?"

"I don't even remember," I tell her honestly. After that final hit of shock, I barely remember the conversation. "Something about me telling him I want to marry him, but not when the motivation is a kneejerk reaction because of his dad."

She nods.

"But does it matter?" I ask, tilting my head back to look at the ceiling to stop the new flood of tears. "I love him, and I want to marry him, so does it really matter what the circumstances are for why we get engaged?" I shake my head. "But, at the same time, if his dad is the motivating factor, and that's the only reason we're getting engaged, then it seems we're going to be starting things off on a terrible foot and will likely have resentment and regret. And maybe it's selfish and childish, but I want more. I want to get engaged because we can't live without each other, because we love each other and are committing to love each other forever. I don't want to marry him because his dad is perpetually unhappy and can't remain monogamous."

Poppy shakes her head and reaches for my hand, holding it between both of hers. "That's not asking for too much. I'm sure Lincoln was being reactive and probably wasn't considering how this could be hurtful to you, but that doesn't mean your feelings aren't valid."

"He seemed really hurt that I said no."

Poppy shakes her head. "That doesn't mean you should have said yes."

Another tear paints a path down my cheek. "What happens next?"

Poppy's hand constricts around mine. "When you're ready, you guys will talk and move forward. Maybe this was good, and it will open the door to discuss the future and what that looks like—what you both want and need."

"You see all of this so clearly, so simply. I wish you'd been there. You could have coached us through it and probably prevented everything."

"No way. It's easy for me to say this *because* I wasn't there. It's different when you're in the moment, especially in your case where you'd been blindsided once by his dad and then a second time by Lincoln's proposal. If that had been Pax and me, I would have been too stunned to think clearly or rationally."

I release a weighted breath, my feelings and thoughts still tangled. "Christmas is in a little more than a week, and then I leave." My vision becomes blurry. "Sometimes, I regret going for my master's. I barely see Lincoln, or you, or my mom—I haven't seen Gramps since Thanksgiving—sometimes I fear that the cost of what I'm losing and missing now may not be worth the future outcomes."

Poppy's gaze is filled with sympathy and compassion. "Being a cetologist has always been your dream, but it's coming at a high price. Could you reduce your credit hours?"

"I'm so close to being done. I don't want to drag it out longer." I scrub at my cheeks, the drying tears causing my skin to itch. "But then, I have to earn my doctorate...." Dread sits on my chest like an elephant—paralyzing me at the reality of four to six additional years of school.

"Let's get in our pajamas. I'll make some hot chocolate, and we'll put on *White Christmas*. You need to decompress and take a break."

I peel off one heel and then the other and dig my toes into the carpet. Rose did an entire seminar once on a technique called "earthing," and Poppy, Olivia, and I had been her practice audience. The process is simple and reminds me of the movie *Die Hard*. Rose had told us that being barefoot outside and connecting with nature had a plethora of health benefits. The rug isn't natural or earthy, yet my shoulders sink, and my breaths feel more level, and while I'm sure it has far more to do with Poppy at my side with a plan and a shoulder to cry on, I put stock into Rose's assurance that being barefoot will help calm me.

"I'm going to try calling Lincoln," I tell her. "I don't know where we left things, and I won't be able to sleep as things stand now."

Poppy nods. "That's probably a good idea."

My bedroom here at the apartment has mainly been unused over the past couple of years. Since Lincoln got his own place, I've spent nearly every night there. As a result, my closet is mostly filled with off-season clothing.

Rather than find something to change into, I sit on the edge of my bed and prepare to call Lincoln, but before I can finish rehearsing what I'll say my phone rings.

6

LINCOLN

I pull up to the marina, where a chained gate stops me. A gate that wasn't here when I'd come by years ago, knowing there was a healthy chance of running into Rae. My headlights shine on the gravel lot, resurfacing so many memories.

My phone ringing interrupts my wandering thoughts before I'm ready. I glance at the screen and see Rae's name. We need to talk through shit, I need to apologize and explain my proposal, and she's going to want to know how I'm feeling about my dad and my new brother. I'm not ready to talk about it, any of it. The sting of rejection is still burning my skin and thoughts, and I haven't even allowed myself to think about my dad.

I decline the call and send her a text.

Me: I'm sorry, I need a little more time.

The dots beside her name appear and then disappear three times, taking me back to the early days of our relationship, back when I was so damn invested in her and so unwilling to risk my friendship with Paxton and my own sanity, having seen my dad serial date and marry women my entire life. During those several months, Rae had censored herself around me, something that drove me irrationally mad. It took months to realize it bothered me so much because she was the one person I wanted to be completely open and honest with me—someone who cared about more than my reputation and football and my potential future.

The same niggling annoyance teases my senses. Later, I'll likely realize how egocentric and unjust I'm acting, but currently, my sanity requires selfishness. I've been contemplating proposing to Raegan for months—years even. There was no singular moment that I knew Rae was the person I wanted to be with. Instead, it was a culmination of moments and events, struggles and triumphs that made me realize I didn't want to be without her—ever.

Questions that have been running through the back of my mind since she responded with a resounding "no" fight to the front of my thoughts as a realization for why her erased messages and why I chose to ignore her call become abundantly apparent—*what next*? When Arlo had been here visiting this past summer, he'd told Pax and me that he was planning to propose to Olivia, and while he was confident she'd say yes, he continued joking around that if she said no, it would be the end because a relationship can't rebound afterward.

My situation is different.

Rae and I are different.

I tell myself this for the hundredth time, though doubt seems to grow with each reminder.

Raegan: I understand. I'll be at the condo.

I sigh, relief coursing through me faster than the regret that chases me like a safety down the field.

THREE HOURS LATER, I return to the parking lot of my building, my thoughts no clearer than they were when I left. I take the elevator up to my condo, my shoulders tense, mood morose. Inside, every light is on, drawing me toward the bedroom where Rae is folding items into a suitcase.

Panic hits me squarely in the chest, right in the spot where she proves I have a heart. "What are you doing?"

Raegan turns, eyes red, cheeks swollen and blotchy. "They've moved up my trip. Apparently, there have been some issues with fishermen and illegal whalers. So they've decided to bump our trip up, hoping our presence will deter them." She saws her lips, a movement she makes when nervous.

"When are you leaving?"

"Sunday."

"Sunday? As in two days from now?"

She glances at the alarm clock shining from the nightstand on my side of the bed that says it's past midnight. "Technically, tomorrow."

"What about Christmas?"

Her eyes swell with tears, but she turns before I can soak in the rest of the details from the single expression. She's guarded, defensive. I know, just like I know she won't say no to them but hates herself over the fact. I know it's unfair that I press her on missing Christmas when I know she wants to be here, but the reminder of her priorities pours salt on my already gaping wound.

"I wish they hadn't moved it. I really wish I could be here for Christmas with you and my family, but I have to complete this research to complete my master's." She says, giving me a proverbial kick to the balls because while I'm feeling unhinged and ready to spar, she's still calm, cool, and rational.

"Hopefully, we'll be able to do a video call," I say, mustering every bit of energy to sound equally composed.

She glances over one shoulder, eyes still glassy with tears, before she faces the bureau, wipes her face, and collects the contents of the drawer. She walks to the foot of the bed where her bag lies open and drops socks and underwear beside a short stack of shorts and T-shirts. "I can finish packing tomorrow. We should get to bed. It's late."

I have a stricter curfew now than when I was in college, one I resent nearly as much as Rae's education taking her away at this moment.

She grabs her suitcase and lowers it to the ground before I can reach her. We stand a foot apart, staring at each other for several minutes before she takes a sidestep and moves into the bathroom, closing the door.

I SHOULD BE EXHAUSTED from lying awake all night, a prisoner to my thoughts, but I'm not. That will likely come tomorrow for game day. I roll over and shut off the alarm before it sounds, so that Rae can sleep in. She rolls over, and I notice the glint of her opened eyes in the darkened room.

I want to ask her if she slept, and if she's feeling as shredded and confused as I am but fuck if I'm not already feeling vulnerable and combative.

"Don't forget to watch for their cornerback," she whispers. "He'll go for your legs." Her concern for me sways me toward her, defying my need to pull away.

I reach forward, grazing her cheek with my fingers. "I will."

"Mom and Pax are still counting on you being there for Christmas. And Gramps and Camilla, too."

We had scheduled to spend Christmas Eve with my dad, Christmas day with her family, and the day after Christmas with my mom.

"I'm going to miss you," I admit, my voice soft, though the words are far from being a secret.

"I'm going to miss you." Her voice cracks, creating a fault line in my chest that violently shifts when she sobs and then shudders.

The doorbell buzzes, and her phone vibrates on the nightstand.

Rae sucks in a breath and gets out of bed. "That's probably Pax."

She reaches for her bra, sitting on the brown leather chair, which is often the target of discarded clothing, and quickly puts it on before heading out of the room.

The door opens, and I hear Pax's greeting and then Poppy's as I pull on my team sweats. I dig for a shirt as Paxton asks Rae about where she'll be, if it will be safe, if she'll have cell reception—all the questions I should have asked.

Pax's gaze lifts to me as I enter the living room, his brows inching higher with a silent question before returning to Rae as she tells him her cell phone reception will likely be spotty and unpredictable, especially out on the ocean. I set down my bag and run a hand through my hair. I had tried to send her with a satellite phone when she went on her first trip into the field, only to have it confiscated because they're heavily regulated, forcing us to rely on shitty reception. Poppy glances at me, trepidation visible, making me question if she knows about last night.

"Do you have everything you need?" Poppy asks, turning her attention to Rae. "Cash, backup chargers, sunscreen? Do we need to go get anything?"

Rae nods, and Poppy does, too. "We'll make a list today and double-check everything."

Again, Rae nods, her cheeks growing red with emotion.

"You need to make sure you have reception on Christmas is all I'm saying," Pax tells her, wrapping an arm around her shoulders and hauling her against his chest. His bottom lip trembles and his eyes turn the same shade of red that Rae's do when she's fighting tears. "Take care of yourself," he says, holding her tight. The redness spreads to his cheeks, and then he dips his face into her shoulder. I've only seen my best friend cry on a handful of occasions, and all but one involved either Rae or their older sister, Maggie, leaving. "I love you."

Raegan's back is to me, but I hear her sniffle. "I love you, too."

They remain in a tight embrace for several long moments before slowly parting. "I'm going to eat all the mashed potatoes at Christmas," Pax tells her as Poppy replaces him.

Rae laughs in return, her arms still bound tight around Poppy. "Camilla's making scalloped potatoes this year."

"What?" Pax objects, but Raegan doesn't respond as she buries her face into Poppy's shoulder.

"I am going to miss you so much," Poppy says. "But you're going to be safe, and do amazing things, and send us all the awesome pictures of whales and dolphins and Christmas with palm trees." Her voice breaks at the end. Pax looks tortured as he looks at them, his own distress growing with Poppy's.

Selfishly, I wish they'd leave. Not only because I want these last few moments for myself, but also because there are so many things Rae and I need to say to each other. Last night, I lay awake, thinking about what she was walking into on her trip. Poachers and illegal whalers had already left scars and a cast on her before, and the idea of her getting involved again had me contemplating excuses for her not to go and preparations for her if she needed help while down there.

Rae keeps one arm around Poppy's waist as the two part. "Make sure you check on Mom. She's been getting down. I think this time of year makes her lonely."

Pax nods, wiping at his eyes with one fist. "I will, and I'll ask how the menu changed."

Rae grins. "You should pay better attention to the family text."

Pax scoffs, shaking his head. "Grandpa sends like two words at a time. It kills me."

Rae grins, wiping at her cheeks with the palms of her hands. "You guys should get going. You're going to be late." She finally turns her attention to me, pain reflecting in her eyes.

Pax nods, the red tint returning to his face. "Let us know when you get there."

Rae nods. "I will."

"And no jumping off any boats or diving without a partner," he adds.

"Done and done."

Pax releases a heavy breath. "And bring me back something cool."

This makes her laugh again, the sound a balm to the emotions that make that fault line in my chest shake again.

"Do you want to ride with me? Poppy's flight isn't until this afternoon." Pax looks at me, and though I want to say no, I recognize he's asking me to be there for him.

I nod, and Raegan smiles at me, one that expresses both relief and gratitude like I answered the question correctly. She walks to where I'm standing, likely realizing I can't move. All my focus is on keeping myself together because though this is the third time she's made one of these trips since being introduced to Dr. Swanson, the marine biologist heading this trip, it's equally hard to say goodbye, harder this time with the turmoil from last night.

She wraps her arms around my waist. "Have fun tomorrow. You're going to do amazing."

I kiss the crown of her head. "Be safe. If you need anything—"

"Call Tyler," Pax interrupts. He shrugs when I cut my attention to him. "Man's got money coming out of his ears, and so many damn connections...." He stops, shrugging again.

Rae fights a smile. "I won't need to call Tyler."

I grab my bag and lean in to kiss her. "I love you."

"I love you, too." Tears swim in her eyes as Poppy stands next to her.

Pax doesn't talk as we take the elevator down to the parking garage, but once we're seated in his car, he turns to me. "Are you okay?"

I nod.

"It sucks she has to leave this close to Christmas."

I nod again.

"At least she'll be back before Vegas and the wedding," he tacks on, putting his car into gear. "Let's go kick some Forty-Niner's ass."

7

LINCOLN

The next thirty-six hours pass in a blur. Nothing is quite right, even during the game. My own body and movements don't feel familiar, and when I return home, the condo doesn't either. I heave a sigh, looking around the space that Rae tidied before leaving. I wish she hadn't—it makes her absence more blatant. I head to the bedroom to put my things down and discover a red gift with a shiny gold bow set on my pillow.

I drop my bag and walk to the edge of the bed to pick up the present. I pluck off the bow, dropping it to the comforter before ripping open the red paper. Inside is *Appian's Roman History*, a note tucked inside the cover.

Merry early Christmas. The rest of your gifts are in the box at the back of the closet, along with everyone else's. Please bring them over with you on Christmas.
Love,
Rae

I lie on my back, turning through the pages written about Ancient

Rome, ignoring the trainer's advice instructing me to take an ice bath and drink my weight in fluids.

A text has me sitting up.

Arlo: I saw you out there tonight, kicking ass!! Go President!

Me: We got lucky.

I got lucky. The only reason we mustered a win was muscle memory and luck.

Arlo: First rule, never admit that to outsiders. ;)

Arlo: How are you doing? How's Rae Rae? We're pumped to see you guys soon. Vegas is going to be lit!

I've never been the conversationalist in our small group. Yet, as we've been stretched across the US, I've worked to be better about casual conversations, realizing these strings of messages are the equivalent of getting a beer and watching a game in the adult version of life.

Me: Rae had to leave early for her trip to Mexico. She left this morning.

Arlo: No wonder you had so much rage on the field.

Arlo: I'm sorry, buddy. That sucks.

Me: How are wedding plans?

The question paints a picture in my head—one of Rae in a white dress, walking down the aisle. I close my eyes, trying to rid the thought as fast as it had appeared.

Arlo: EXPENSIVE!! When you and Rae are ready to tie the knot, do a destination wedding. Fly to Hawaii, get married on the beach, stay at the fanciest hotel, and you'll save so much money!

I think of the details that Arlo's texted to Pax or myself over the past months, the ice bar he plans to have, the dance floor that lights under everyone's feet, the massive tents. The wedding will be a show, primarily conducted by Arlo, whose only response is that he's only getting married once.

Me: How's the knee?

I veer our conversation away from weddings and the jealousy that prods my memories as I recall Rae giving me a resounding *"no,"* the look of confusion and hurt on her face.

Arlo: It's mostly fine. Occasionally, I'll feel some pain when I plant and cut, but it's been good.

Me: Glad to hear it. Some days, this job makes me feel old.

Arlo: Don't tell Rose that. She'll give you an entire yoga routine to practice.

I grin, recalling Thanksgiving, and Rose convincing Pax, Ian, and me to try some yoga with her. She hadn't suggested it with tales of it helping us or trying to sell any benefits. Instead, Rose went straight for the jugular—our pride—telling us she bet we couldn't do it. Little did she know that I began doing yoga last year. Most of the team does. We even have an instructor on staff.

Both parties were left surprised: us that she had the strength and balance of an acrobat and her, that we didn't kill ourselves trying to replicate her moves.

Arlo: I've got to hit the hay, but Liv and I are excited to see you in a few weeks when we come to visit. Take care of yourself, and if you get bored, my phone is always on me. I love you, man.

Arlo's still one of the best people I've ever had the benefit of knowing.

Me: I'm sending you big, full-frontal hugs.

Arlo: Yeah, man. That's the only way we hug around here.

I chuckle as I set my phone down, debating eating something and deciding to shower instead to get off all the product our trainer rubbed over my shoulder and calves after our win.

The last time Rae left for one of these trips, we were mid-season, and while I missed her like crazy, football kept me busy and, therefore, sane. I wish that were the scenario now because, in another week, I will have entirely too much time on my hands.

I towel off and pull on a clean pair of boxer briefs before pulling the bedding back to lie down. Tomorrow's a rest day, but I'll still have to go to the practice facility. My phone flips with the movement, the light alerting me of a notification. I reach for it, expecting another text from Arlo, and see two missed calls from an unknown number and one voicemail.

"Hey, it's me. I'm calling you on a radio phone because we don't seem to have any reception. There was a storm, so I'm hoping that's why, and it will be restored soon. Anyways, I just want to let you know I arrived, and they only lost one of my bags this time." She laughs quietly, a forced sound. "Luckily, I learned from last time to pack extra underwear in my carry-on." She's rambling, a sure sign that she's nervous. "I'll try calling again soon. I hope your game and trip went well. I love you."

The message ends too soon. I wish it went on for hours because just the sound of her voice calms and settles the restless unease that lives inside of me.

I turn my ringer up as loud as it will go, set it by my pillow, and fall asleep.

————

I MISS Rae's next call two days later due to a meeting that goes long. Her message is again brief, with lots of noise in the background and the promise to call again soon. Practice keeps me busy, but my thoughts stray, leading to stupid mistakes that have Coach on my ass. His efforts on me are misplaced and futile because this week's game is against the Broncos, and if we had Pax, we'd stand a chance, but we're hopeless without him. Yet, I welcome the anger and drive that carries me to the weekend. The game is a battle of wills and strength, resulting in a loss by three, which almost feels like a win.

THE FOLLOWING week and a half bleed together until Christmas, one of the few days we have off during the season. My email confirms that Rae received the flowers I had delivered to her yesterday, but her gifts sit on the top shelf of my closet, still unwrapped. I'd been too stunned by her news of leaving to connect the dots that she wouldn't be here, and with her having strict limitations for her baggage, I wouldn't have been able to send her gifts even if I'd been lucid enough.

The fact that Rae promised to call on Christmas is what has me showing up to her mom's house as planned. Cole answers the door. In the years that I've known him, the only thing that's changed about their grandfather is his hair has gone nearly entirely white. He's still active, stubborn, and the backbone of the family.

"Merry Christmas," he says, pulling me in for a hug. "You had another great game this last weekend," he says, patting my shoulder as I step into the house. He gestures to the flower arrangements I'm holding with an approving grin.

The room, which had been purple for an entire year, is now a light shade of gray. A tall, narrow Christmas tree is set up behind the couch, towering nearly to the ceiling, adorned with red and gold ornaments.

"Hey, man," Pax calls from the kitchen. A few years ago, the two of us knocked down the wall that separated the two rooms, making it one large space.

Camilla, Rae's and Paxton's step-grandma, Deborah, their mom, and Poppy all turn to welcome me with a chorus of Merry Christmases.

I've been dreading this day, convinced the holiday would be awkward and that I'd be an outsider. I should have known better because even before Rae and I began dating, I've always felt welcomed by her family. We spend the day watching football, eating trays of appetizers, playing card games that Deborah stacked on the table, and drinking eggnog and mimosas that Poppy created using orange juice and sparkling cider.

It's the first time I've felt like myself since that hellish night with my dad. My shoulders finally don't feel tight, my mood is calm and easy, and when my thoughts shift to Rae, the doubt isn't as loud. It's like a rainstorm has slowed to a drizzle, the proverbial clouds parting, and then a knock on the door has us all turning in our seats.

Paxton beams, and Deborah wears a matching smile. My chest constricts, hope growing like an avalanche, knocking the rest of my doubts and fears out of the way.

Pax stands, and all our eyes follow him to the door. I'm so damn sure Rae's going to walk through that I'm ready to bet my career on the fact. But when Pax opens the door, an anvil falls on me like that old cartoon, as Poppy's parents and little brother appear.

"You guys came!" Poppy cries. "I thought you were driving to Medford to see Grandma?"

My shoulders tense—my entire body does. Intuition tells me whatever is coming will burn, but my loyalty keeps me rooted in place as Paxton drops to one knee and slides a jewelry box from his pocket.

Poppy gasps, and I can't stop myself from watching her reactions like it's a movie playing in slow motion. She covers her mouth with both hands as her eyes well with tears that she blinks away, and though she's still covering her mouth, her eyes are smiling.

"We started as friends, and then you became my fake girlfriend to help save me from myself. But we both know there was never anything fake between us. You are the most real and honest part of my life. You make me want to be a better son, friend, teammate, and brother—a better everything. You make me complete. And I promise to be the best version of myself, and to love you, and cook for you—" quiet laughter spreads through the house, "—for the rest of my life. And I would be so honored if you would be my life partner and wife."

Poppy wipes at the tears that have appeared on her face, her smile radiating, saying her answer before she nods and cries out a "Yes!"

The games end, and the conversations and jokes are forgotten, replaced with talk about the engagement. And no matter how hard I try to stop feeling like an asshole and celebrate my best friend's happiness, a bitter and jealous energy steals the rest of the day from me.

————

I'VE SPOKEN to Rae three times in the past week, all of them brief. Between practice and her being out on the ocean most days, we're having a difficult time connecting. We knew we would. We've played this song and dance before, which is partly why I've been dreading this trip, though I've tried to remain optimistic about it, keeping my objections to myself.

Our game this week is another away game, this one taking us to Oklahoma City. I finish packing my suitcase and am about to turn on some tape to study some final details in preparations for Sunday's game when my doorbell rings.

Rae and Paxton are the only two with keys, and they're also the only two who come over, which has me reaching for a shirt since I hadn't donned one since showering.

I swing open the door and find a woman with shoulder-length dark hair and a scattered expression that seemingly clears as she

looks up at me. "I'm so sorry to bother you. I live right down there—"
she points at the end of the hall, which curves before the next condo,
"—my cat got loose. Gray, super fluffy, kind of looks like she was elec-
trocuted fluffy. Flat face. Any chance you've seen her?" She has to
look up at me because she's so short, barely over five feet.

I shake my head.

"Shoot. Thanks for your time. Sorry I bothered you." She takes a
step, then stops, looking over her shoulder at me. "Would you mind
helping me look? She's skittish, and I'm worried she might run in the
opposite direction if someone opens their door. I promise I'll only
take a few more minutes of your time."

I scrub a hand over my face. "Sure. Want me to stay here in case
she comes back this way? Or go down to the entrance?"

"The entrance, please. Maybe we'll find her on our way down the
stairs." She starts toward the hallway to our left, in the direction of
the stairs. "By the way, I'm Natalie."

"Lincoln," I tell her, following the stairs. I always take the elevator,
traveling between the garage and my condo.

"I've seen a girl stop at your condo a few times. Blonde hair, black
bag, wears a blue coat a lot. Is she your cleaning lady? I really need to
find a cleaning lady."

My eyebrows furrow as I shake my head. "She's my girlfriend,"
I say.

Natalie's jaw falls open. "I didn't mean that offensively."

She did. Maybe not intentionally, but her assumption was steeped
in judgment.

Natalie looks at me and clears her throat. "I haven't seen her in a
while."

"She's saving the world."

Natalie belts out a laugh. "Don't tell me she's Supergirl."

"Cape and everything," I say.

She looks over her shoulder at me, her smile verging on devious.
"So, if I pushed you over the stairwell, would she catch you?"

I'm nearly twice this girl's size, but the terms crazy and toxic are beginning to nest their way into my brief memory of her. "Are you sure your cat got out? Or did you cook it in a stew?"

She laughs too hard. "Have you ever owned a cat? They'll kill you before you kill them. Trust me."

I snigger. Trust and stranger are two words that don't associate themselves in my vocabulary. I'm not nearly as bad as Tyler when it comes to assuming bad intentions, but since being drafted and having more people recognize me, I've been reminded of the ugly sides of fame and money.

"Oh, there she is," Natalie says. A large gray cat stretches nearly the length of a stair, peeking up at us as we draw near.

I stop in case the cat truly is skittish, and Natalie wriggles her fingers and makes kissing sounds at the cat before capturing her with a grunt.

When we reach the hallway to my condo, Natalie releases a heavy breath. "Thanks for your help. I'll see you and Supergirl around."

I head back into my condo without a reply to the strange situation. Inside, I pat my pockets, searching for my cellphone. Being around others only makes me miss Raegan more, and right now, I don't care if my pride is hurt or that I fear she'll never want to marry me. I just need to talk to her, hear her voice, and gain some sanity. My phone isn't on my body, leading me to retrace my steps to my bed, where I find it on the comforter, green light flashing. Two missed calls from Rae.

Son of a fucking electrocuted-looking cat.

I call her back, but it goes directly to voicemail.

The days begin to bleed together again, patched together with practices, workouts, and meetings that aren't nearly as strenuous or demanding after our final game.

8

RAEGAN

Five weeks later

I stand in front of the three-paneled mirror, my thoughts everywhere else but in this moment where they should be, celebrating with two of my best friends as we embark on a new adventure: learning the rules of adulthood.

Eight months ago, Arlo popped the question to Olivia, proposing to her at the end of their vacation to Hawaii.

So many things have happened—so many changes. I wish I had known then how fast time would go and had chosen to ignore my phone and the perceptions of others and had instead been present in every single second of my first two years of college, before Lincoln, Pax, Ian, Rose, Olivia, and Arlo all graduated, tipping the first domino of changes that hit our closely-knit group.

"Rae, you look stunning," Poppy tells me as she comes out of her changing room, wearing an identical Tiffany blue gown. She steps beside me, her long red hair pulled back into an elegant twist that shows off the pearl earrings Pax got her for her birthday last month. My gaze drops to the engagement ring on her left hand, the solitaire that she twists to the inside of her palm when I'm near in an attempt to spare my feelings. I'd thought the ring was too big and didn't fit, twisting due to the weight, until I noticed her doing it intentionally whenever I was around.

"You're so tan," she continues. "You make me look pasty."

My gaze jumps back to my reflection. I returned home from Mexico three days ago, and I wish I were still there in some ways. I missed home, I missed Poppy and my family, I missed simple things like the chill that accompanies winter here, and Christmas, my bed, and hot showers, but more than anything, I missed Lincoln. However, the tension that existed between us prior to me leaving was a fraction of what it's become. Since I've been home, we're both walking on eggshells, timid with each other and distant. I don't want to talk much about my trip, and he's barely spoken about the time that I was gone.

"I'm not that tan," I say, and I'm not. Most of my time there was spent in wet suits or the lab. "And this color looks fantastic with your eyes," I point out.

"This trip is going to be so good for all of us," Poppy says. "We'll have a chance to reconnect, and have fun, and relax. We've all been so busy; this will be a good timeout. And Arlo's family sounds hilarious. The pranks they pull on each other, and the jokes.... We're going to have a great time."

A smile edges its way onto my face, curving my lips as warm memories flood my thoughts of the early years of college when Arlo played a constant role in my life. Arlo and Olivia come back to Seattle the most often since Olivia's family still lives here.

Rose steps out from behind a curtain. "It's so tight it makes me look like I have a uni-boob," she says, moving forward in her heels and climbing the stairs to stand on my other side. Rose is gorgeous. Her honesty and directness are two of the strengths I admire most. She is my reminder that vulnerabilities don't make us weak because she's one of the strongest people I know and is the first to admit her faults and fears. "Are your dresses trying to strangle you?"

"Like a boa constrictor," I admit.

Rose shakes her head. "Your boobs look amazing. Why do mine look like I've duct taped them in place?" She looks down at the dress, pulling at the fabric for a moment before looking at me again. "Lincoln is going to flip out seeing you in that dress." Her smile is knowing and proud.

Poppy looks at me, no doubt waiting for my response. There are few things harder than keeping secrets from your best friend, especially when your best friend is so perceptive.

"Speaking of which, I need your input on Vegas. I want the bachelor and bachelorette party to be epic. I definitely think we need to hire strippers."

"I thought no strippers was one of the contingencies?" Poppy asks, glancing at me for confirmation.

Rose's smile is devious. "It was, but if we're all together with the strippers, no one can get jealous because everyone will know what's happening." She looks from Poppy's doubtful expression to mine, which likely illustrates the same suspicions. "Come on. Strippers can be sexy."

"Maybe we should ask Olivia?" Poppy suggests.

"Or find a Vegas show. I've heard some of them can be really sexy, and then they're on stage, no . . . touching and stuff."

Rose's smile borders on patronizing. "Come on, guys. We're confident in our relationships and our own bodies, and we know that our guys won't cheat. It would just be for fun."

"I'm not worried about Pax cheating. I just don't really like the idea of him getting excited about someone else's naked body," Poppy says.

I shake my head. "And I don't like the idea of my brother getting...." I swallow and shake my head again. "*Excited*." I cringe as I say the word.

Rose belts out a laugh. "Just think about it. We would do it tastefully. It would be art."

I glance from Poppy to Rose, my lips curved with a smile. "We love your confidence and complete lack of prudeness."

Rose tugs at her dress again. "Corrupting my friends, one at a time." She sighs, releasing the fabric. "Besides, those were the dating playbook rules. We're now entering a new set of rules. Marriage rules.

I am willing to bet a thousand dollars another duo from our group will be engaged before the end of the year."

My face warms.

"I'm so glad you and Pax decided to get married this summer," she says, turning to Poppy. "A June wedding is going to be perfect."

Poppy sighs. "I kind of feel like I'm missing a step," she admits. "I still can't find a job. I can't even find a steady substitute teaching gig."

Mom tried finding her work within the school district she is a superintendent for, but there's currently a surplus of teachers, many with more experience and tenure than Poppy.

"You've been helping your mom with the domestic violence project," I interject before she can dismiss the years of work under her belt.

"Do tell," Rose says.

"It's just an idea my mom and I had," Poppy says dismissively.

"A brilliant idea," I add. "They recognized how few know what a healthy relationship looks like or feels like, and what the warning signs are that you might be in an unhealthy or unsafe relationship, and they started putting together a curriculum to educate people on this as well as how to be a good partner. It will be so valuable." I look at Poppy, making sure she hears every word of my compliment.

"That's badass," Rose says, echoing my thoughts. "You're teaching them to swim and CPR for a relationship. Badass," she repeats.

"Thank you," Poppy says, cheeks flushed a light shade of pink.

I glance at the clock that reminds me I'm running late. "Shoot. I've got to get going." I gather the hem of my dress and quickly make my way down the stairs and close the dressing room curtain with a *snap*.

"I'll be at my dad's and Whitney's, but we should go to dinner tomorrow for our last night," Rose says. "Bring Pax and Lincoln. I haven't seen them since our belated Thanksgiving."

I shuck off the dress and carefully hang it back up. "Lincoln's been really busy working with the coaches," I explain, sliding on my leggings.

"Tell him to take the night off or face the wrath of Ian and Rose."

I wrestle on my shirt, socks, and shoes before facing the narrow mirror, catching sight of the scar that runs along the side of my forearm where I'd cut myself while saving Blue, the bottlenose dolphin I see once a week in the Puget Sound. My thoughts flash to that first night when Lincoln had seen the scar, back when the skin was purple and angry, back when we were fighting to both stay apart and remain together. Now, the line is pale and flat, a whisper of my past.

The dull ache in my chest grows, and my eyes gloss with tears. I release a shallow breath, and then another. "I can't make any promises," I say, taking another breath, this one clearer. I double-check that my mascara hasn't strayed and then grab my purse and bridesmaid dress, leaving the confines of the small room. "But I'll definitely be there."

Poppy's green eyes are focused on me, critical and intrusive, but I have the excuse of work.

"Text or call me with details, and I'll see you tomorrow."

"I will. Love you, Rae," Rose says, reaching for me. She hugs me tight, her dress is scratchy against my bare arms. "Where's your coat? It's freezing outside."

"I have one in my car," I lie as she releases me. I turn to Poppy. "I'll probably be home late, so if I don't see you tonight, I'll see you tomorrow."

She fiddles with her earring but reluctantly nods. "Love you."

I grin. "I love you both. Drive safe. Have fun!"

The February air chills me, sending a shiver down my spine. The sky is an endless gray canvas, and the area of town we're in is industrial, the buildings all concrete and white, blending into the skyline. I don't mind the winter months in Seattle that often stretch far into spring, but today they feel taxing.

I slip the finished dress into my trunk and sit in my car; my thoughts numb as I try to keep myself from considering tomorrow night or Vegas or Arlo and Olivia's wedding.

I enter the directions to the aquarium, put the car into gear, and drive to work.

I step through the doors, expecting the energy and peace that generally greets me at the door, but am instead greeted by a loud sigh coming from April, one of our volunteers.

"Long day?" I ask.

She gives me a silent look that confirms it has. "I have a feeling it's going to be a long quarter. Why do people love their straws so much?"

I wince at the reminder that comes from her question. This year, our focus at the aquarium is educating visitors about plastics and their harm to the ocean and, therefore, animals. "I wish straws were the greatest worry," I say, taking a seat at the table in our break room as Greta enters, wearing her customary blue sweatshirt. While in Mexico, we went out daily for weeks to work on a floating heap of plastic, that like most of the garbage in our ocean, was caused by fishermen. Commercial fishing nets, plastic crates, ropes, eel trap cones, and oyster spacers were a primary source of danger to the marine life in the area.

Greta steps closer. "We have to remember that we're not here to shame people or argue with anyone. My mom still insists on using straws every day." She shakes her head. "All we can do is help shine a light on this problem because as we continue in this direction, there will be more plastic than fish in our oceans, and it won't take long to get there. We all have to do our part. My mom still uses straws but now uses reusable grocery bags and gets her soap refills from a company that mails them to her in fully recyclable cardboard containers, and she's so proud of herself. She sends me a picture of them every time she gets an order." Greta smiles affectionally. "No one's perfect, and we don't need anyone to be perfect, just aware."

And with her short speech, Greta reminds me why I love working here so much.

I spend most of my shift in the back with our traveling veterinarian, who I now assist with most procedures. Today, we're treating a sea otter brought in with a wound to its flank that ends up being from a BB gun. We pull out three bullets and sew him up before giving him an IV of antibiotics and fluids.

· · ·

AFTER MY SHIFT, I head to the condo. For the past several years, this has been my norm. This same time last year, I'd be walking into the condo, and Lincoln would pause whatever he was doing. I'd peel off my shirt and toss it at him and continue to the bedroom, losing articles of clothing along the way like I was peeling off the day and starting anew with Lincoln, naked in his bed, where pleasure and release were the only things we'd seek.

Now, my thoughts are in overdrive, an old habit that rarely involves Lincoln anymore because my feelings and confidence in our relationship have been so solid. It's amazing how one conversation, one question—or perhaps one answer—has led to so much instability.

I take the elevator up to the condo, and debate pretending like these invisible hurdles that keep tripping us up aren't there. If I do what I'd just imagined and tear my clothes off, will it snap everything back to normal like hitting a reset button?

Determination warms my blood as I unlock the door, preparing to straddle him right on the couch, but my idea dies a quick death as I swing the door open to an empty space. My shoulders fall, and fear knots in my belly. He's been gone more than usual since I've been back, filling his time off with additional workouts and preparing for Paxton's first year as the quarterback.

I head to the bedroom, placing my work clothes into the hamper and pulling on a warm hoodie and jeans before heading to my mom's.

Gramps sits in the armchair, watching a movie when I arrive, a bowl of popcorn on his lap. "Hey, hey! Look who the cat dragged in," he says, sitting up. "I thought you were coming over tomorrow?" He sets the bowl on the coffee table and stands, pulling me into a much-needed hug. His shaved cheek is rough against mine, and he smells of the same coffee and clean laundry. "We missed you." He holds on longer, his actions matching the sentiment.

"I missed you, too. How have things been?"

He nods a couple of times. "We finished the back garden while you were gone."

"You did?" I glance toward the kitchen that opens to the backyard, where Mom and Gloria, Lincoln's childhood nanny, who is still employed for Lincoln's father, had masterminded the plan. My thoughts wander to Lincoln's little brother, Maverick, and I wonder if Gloria knows about him. If she's caring for him?

"Lincoln and Paxton came over, and we got the rest of it done. Go take a look."

Conflict settles in my chest. It feels like Lincoln is pulling away, and the distance between us is growing, but reminders and actions like this—him helping my family, spending Christmas with them—contradict my uncertainties.

I cross the space and open the back door leading to a concrete slab with a large overhang. The yard is primarily a large hill, something Mom was okay with because she's never cared about having a big backyard, but Pax was concerned that a rainstorm could cause the dirt to flood toward the house. Grandpa seconded the worry, and they had a retaining wall put in during her first summer. Mom was going to leave the sloped side of the yard alone and wild and stick to growing the small herb garden with Gloria's expertise near the patio. That tiny garden became an obsession for Mom, and last year she decided to have the hill made into a garden, realizing that while knitting was never her strong suit, she had two green thumbs.

Gramps, Paxton, and Lincoln helped with some of the work, the other part contracted out, but last October, while the weather was unusually warm and dry, Poppy, Mom, Camilla, and I began making the backyard an extension of her house. Pax, Lincoln, and Grandpa quickly came to our aid, adding more lights, a porch swing, clearing the hill and tiering it. The backyard has been completely transformed, unrecognizable from the pile of dirt and weeds it once was. Now, everything is wood and stone, with attractive lights, a stone fireplace, oversized furniture, and a table big enough to fit all of us and then some. The terraced garden is bare, the slate walls that separate each level exposed. A set of stairs runs down the middle, and light posts stand at the edge of each pathway.

"This is amazing," I say, tracking over the details again. "You guys did such a great job."

Gramps smiles his approval. "Camilla and Poppy did most of the directing. We were just the muscle." He flexes and then winces.

I give him a courtesy laugh, appreciating his efforts to make me smile. "I bet Mom freaked out. Where is she? Is she hiding back there?"

Gramps motions with a thumb at the ceiling. "She had a work call."

"Has she been swamped, still?"

He lifts his silver brows. "You know how she is. If she's not busy, she finds more work." He gently prods me with his elbow. "That trait rubbed off on you. Come on. I'll show you how to be lazy. Let's order some pizza, then you can tell me about your trip."

"Where's Camilla?" I ask, following him back into the living room. This house was once filled with projects and felt almost like a place-holder, so different from my childhood home. As a family, we've been tackling them, transforming the house into a home. It still looks very different from the old house—something I think Mom chose inten-tionally when picking out colors and furniture—but it still reflects her, and so many details hold memories from us working on them that it feels homey.

"She should be here soon. She had a meeting at the church." Gramps sits in the recliner, one of the few pieces that Mom brought with her from the old house. I sit on the sectional, tucking my feet underneath me. "Hey, kiddo," he says, drawing my attention to him. "Is everything okay?"

"Yeah," I say, trying to sound convincing for my benefit as well as his. "I'm just adjusting to being back and school."

He nods. "Kick your feet up, and rest while I order the pizza." He grabs his reading glasses from the table beside his chair and slides them on so he can see the screen of his phone, and proceeds to order. "Is Lincoln coming? I want to make sure we have enough since that boy can eat an entire pizza by himself."

"Let me check."

Maybe it's my own guilt, but I swear Gramps raises his eyebrows like he's surprised by my response. Lincoln and I aren't glued at the hip. We have never been because we've never been able to, yet, because of how busy our schedules are, we've always been very transparent about plans so we can find whatever time to steal together, so we always seem to know where the other one is.

> **Me: Hey. I stopped at my mom's to visit, and Gramps is here. Camilla is on the way. Do you want to come over for pizza?**

> **Lincoln: Sorry, I can't. I have a meeting with Coach here in 10. I'll see you when I get home.**

"He has a meeting," I say, relaying the message to Gramps.

Gramps reaches across the space, laying his hand atop mine. "Tell me about Mexico."

"It was pretty amazing. There have been times in the past year and a half, working for my master's, where it seems like it's too late for us to make a difference and help the marine animals, and we're destined to this fate that the past wrote for us. Professors and books give us stats and data points that seem like doom and gloom, and I know it's real. We have a lot to achieve to make a change. But at the same point, getting out there and seeing some of the ways people are working to clean the oceans and preserve wildlife is so inspiring. This trip really recharged my battery and helped me remember why I love cetology so much. Also, wait till I show you this video. You're going to lose your dentures."

Grandpa chuckles. "Try me."

I scroll through my pictures, selecting the right video before tilting my phone for Gramps to watch the baby humpback whale, which was at least twenty-five feet long, swim under the small paddleboard I was on.

Gramps shakes his head. "Nope. Not a chance. If I had dentures to lose, I'd have lost them. Did you show that to your mom? Better yet, did you show it to Lincoln?" He shakes his head. "He's going to tie you to a chair the next time you tell him you want to go out on one of these trips."

My smile is contrived because I haven't shown Lincoln the video. We've barely spoken about the trip or his work.

"What kind of pizza did you order?" I ask, changing the subject.

9

LINCOLN

Our breaks are split up between three allotments, all during the spring, to ensure the team remains in shape and doesn't do anything too stupid or crazy. It's apparent everyone is looking forward to our first break because now, when stupid mistakes are made during practice, most of the team remains in a good mood. Rae has been home for a week, and things are still off between us. When she bobs, I weave, and vice versa. This weekend, I'm hoping Vegas is our silver bullet.

Paxton has officially begun training as our quarterback, which has changed another dynamic of our team, his demeanor a drastic change from Brevard, who has officially retired. The team likes Pax— some of them respect him, others don't realize how good he is and are underestimating his abilities as both a player and leader. He's taking it in stride.

I shift the weight of the box one of our publicists sent me home with, filled with jerseys I need to finish signing as I try to unlock my door.

"Hey, neighbor," Natalie says as she turns down the hallway, grocery sacks filling her arms. "Tell me you have a gym addiction without telling me you have a gym addiction." Her gaze drops to my duffle bag. Since her cat got loose, I've seen her a handful of times, always in the hall, paired with a sarcastic retort and a smile.

I tip the box too far as I twist the key, and a small pile of jerseys falls to the floor.

Natalie sets her bags down and grabs the offending articles of clothing, holding one up to examine it. "I thought you looked familiar," she says, smiling at me. She glances at the jerseys again and then slings one over her shoulder and drops the rest back into my box. "Finder's fee," she says with a smile as she lowers to gather her groceries again. As she lifts them, an orange drops, rolling toward my feet.

I push open my door and drop the box inside to prop it open for me as I retrieve her orange.

"I'm not sure if my produce is attacking you or just knows it will fall to its doom and rot in a bowl if it goes home with me."

I take two short steps, but before I can return it, she twists. "Consider it your finder's fee," she says, then winks and heads down the hall. "See you later, Lincoln."

I kick the box further inside the condo and drop my bag to the floor. The team wasn't focusing, so Coach told us to go home and take a break. It's the first time he's done this, but I'm hoping it's not the last because sometimes just stepping outside of the facility eases the pressure and helps me remember why I love this sport and how damn much I love my job.

I glance at my phone to check the time and determine where Rae is. I text her to let her know practice will likely go late because of our unforeseen break. I sit back, peering around at the condo, trying to determine what in the hell to do with my time when there's a knock on the door.

I climb to my feet and open the door to find Gloria on the opposite side.

"You're about two months too late," I tell her.

Her shoulders sink, and I hate myself a little for the quip, though I make no attempt to take it back. Gloria's on my shortlist of people I trust and those I care for. The fact that she didn't give me a heads up or tell me about my father's affair and the child that came with it feels like an act of betrayal.

"You know why I couldn't tell you."

I shake my head. "No, but I know why you *should* have told me. You let me walk right into a trap, completely blindsided."

Gloria puts her hands on her hips, her marred expression equal parts determination and regret. "We need to talk. Let's go inside."

"I don't have anything to talk about."

"Well, I do." She pushes past me into the condo.

I let the door close behind her and pull in a deep breath. These days, my patience doesn't have the same hair-trigger, but right now, it feels alarmingly short.

"You and your dad have always had a tempestuous relationship. It's like you speak two different languages. He had to be the one who told you about Carol, and Tara, and Maverick."

I nod. "And meanwhile, I'm assuming you've been raising their child."

"Maverick," she repeats his name. "You always wanted a brother."

Her reminder feels like an accusation and betrayal delivered in one swift blow. "When I was *six*."

"He isn't to blame for the situation."

I run my hands through my hair, fighting to remain calm. Gloria's seen me at my worst, but I still hate how vulnerable I feel. I loathe that my dad's decisions impact me. "Why are you here?"

"Because you keep ignoring all my calls and messages."

"I told you, I don't have anything to say."

"Your dad messed up taking you to dinner and dropping the news on you like that. I had no idea that was how he planned to tell you. But you know him. He hates confrontation, and you never run from it."

"Now it's my fault?"

"You never liked Carol. I don't understand why this time is different. Why are you so angry this time?"

"Why are you defending him?"

"Because the women in your dad's life have never mattered, but this is different. You now have a family. A brother."

"Right. My dad's second chance."

Hurt resonates in her eyes. This conversation would be so much easier if she replied with frustration and disappointment—anger—anything but sympathy and compassion. "I know this is hard for you. Your dad was barely around when you were a child, and he rarely played or showed interest in the things you loved. It took him over twenty years to recognize that, and now, he finally wants to do a better job and offer Maverick the love and support he never knew how to provide you with."

Something in my chest feels raw, everything too tight. "Gloria, he had an affair! *Another* affair, *another* failed marriage. Chances are, this one will go to shit as well, and you'll never see the kid because you know him—you know he's not going to change."

"He's been to every one of your home games since you started playing for the Seahawks. People can change, but you have to allow them to and believe in them."

I scoff, shaking my head, dismissing her eternal faith in my father. "You've always believed he was better than he really is."

"It was just easier for me to see his love for you because I wasn't the one disappointed and failed. He didn't love you as you needed and wanted—like every child needs to be loved with affection, care, and patience. He didn't know how to do that for you or your mother, but he did it in the best way he knew how and that was by working and providing for you."

My resentment is a shallow grave because I didn't have a bad childhood. I had plenty of attention thanks largely to my mom and Gloria, but hearing her defend my dad, knowing he wasn't an active participant in most of my life, grinds my gears.

"He wants to change, and now you have a little brother, and while he'll likely be closer to your kids than he'll be to you, he's your blood —family."

"You're not my blood, and you're family."

Her gaze falls as she makes a quiet sigh, a smile capturing her mouth. When she looks back at me, her eyes are filled with tears as she nods. "Yes." Her voice is shaky. "But I made my fair share of mistakes with you as well. You were just quicker to forgive me."

I start to object, but she holds up a hand.

"Your dad loves you, he's just never known how to show it. And now you're a man, a better man than he was at this age—and he knows that. You have Raegan, your dream career, friends, and you know your priorities, something it took him most of his life to figure out. Your dad has always been intimidated by your fierce independence and determination. Failure has never been an option for you. But he's been trying to change and improve and show you a better side of him, but you refuse to allow him to. Instead, you keep him in the same box of who he was throughout your childhood."

"I don't understand why you're here condemning me when he had another affair and introduced me to her and their byproduct in the middle of a steakhouse with no warning. That's not changing. That's not admitting his faults or being held accountable."

"Do you think he wasn't embarrassed and intimidated to admit to his perfect son who has a perfect life that he messed up?"

I breathe out a heavy sigh. "Don't make this my fault. Since that night, everything has gone to shit. I keep trying to convince myself that his choices and decisions don't impact me, and yet they keep defining every part of my life...." I stop, recognizing that I sound like a petulant child. What has happened since that dinner can't be blamed on him, just like a butterfly moving its wings can't cause a tornado—they can just contribute to the storm, and my dad's surprise certainly contributed to the shitshow that happened that night. "I'm not in the right mindset to have this discussion."

Gloria smiles again. "You have grown into a man to be proud of. Your dad doesn't define you—your actions do. You've always followed your heart and dreams. His mistake isn't yours to bear, and you don't have to worry about repeating his mistakes. I'm here, requesting that you recognize this rare opportunity. You don't have to forgive your father and his absences for his benefit—do it for your own, so you're not holding on to that anger and fear."

Gloria stays until I have to return to practice, only for the first time in my pro career, I don't go. I send Rae a text and head off with Gloria's assurance that I'm not my dad playing in my thoughts like a mantra.

Raegan

My stomach protests as I plop down on the couch. I need to eat something, but my feet are sore from walking all day.

My phone buzzes with a text, and I reach for it, hoping the message is from Lincoln, telling me he's on his way home. He messaged me earlier saying he wanted to spend time together, and since reading it, I've been overly hopeful that it's a step toward normalcy.

Poppy: Two days until Vegas!!! What are you packing? Am I supposed to only bring dresses? Are shorts okay? Will I need pants?

Me: No. Yes. Maybe.

Poppy: Where's your enthusiasm?

Me: It's tired.

Poppy: You definitely need to pack that black dress you bought—the one with the see-through parts.

Me: That dress is officially cursed. I wore it the night we went to dinner with Lincoln's dad.

Poppy: That dress deserves a second chance. It's sooooo pretty.

A knock on the door has me looking that way and gauging how many steps I'll have to take.

Me: If you're at the door, use your key.

Poppy: ???

I quietly groan as I get to my feet, tucking my phone into my back pocket before looking through the peephole. On the other side stands an unfamiliar face, a woman with dark hair, adorable freckles, and a smile as she holds something in both hands.

I pull the door open, and my heart stops when I notice her shirt is a Seahawks jersey and not any Seahawks jersey, but one with Lincoln's number on it.

"Hi...." Her voice is too cheerful and loud. I'd bet my car she wasn't expecting me to answer the door. "I'm the neighbor," she says, tacking on a quiet laugh. "I saw Lincoln a couple of hours ago, and he seemed like he was having a bad day, so I was just dropping off these cookies I baked."

On another day, in another setting, I'd focus on why she was baking things for my boyfriend, but a more prudent question has my thoughts arrested. "He hasn't been home. He has late practice today."

The woman shakes her head. "I ran into him in the hallway like ninety minutes ago, and my orange tried attacking him." She laughs again and extends the plate piled with cookies.

I take them and am still standing there dumbstruck as she waves and bids me goodbye.

I go back to the couch and set the cookies down, reaching for my phone.

Poppy: Who stopped by this late? Doesn't everyone know that we stopped hanging out past 6 pm when we hit 22?

Me: Is Pax home?

Poppy: Yeah. Do you need to talk to him?

Instead of replying, I flip from our text thread to Lincoln and mines, rereading the messages he sent earlier to ensure I read them correctly.

Lincoln: Practice is going to run late tonight. Everyone's fucking off.

And then a second sent an hour later.

Lincoln: Can we hang out tonight? Just the two of us. It feels like it's been forever.

I read it twice, tears clouding my vision. Then, I look around, stopping on an orange on the kitchen counter. I still cry when I'm frustrated, but these tears are more insistent, the kind that doesn't creep up and make your eyes itch, but the ones that flood and fall from your eyelids before you've even processed their existence—the broken-hearted variety.

10

RAEGAN

Rather than face Lincoln and the onslaught of questions and emotions that have built up like a dam over the past week and a half, I choose to go back to my apartment and gain a little space and perspective.

Thursday is easy to avoid him. Between packing, laundry, school, and lab, my day is full without any unnecessary excuses, neither of which is actively trying to steal or buy time.

Within forty-eight hours, my pain has manifested into anger, which feels mildly better than sadness. Angry tears dry faster.

This situation conflict is worse than a fight because I don't know where things stand between us. Is he mad at me? Does that girl mean something to him? All I know is that I need to make some big decisions that will come with even bigger feelings, and I don't want to face that this weekend while we're all in Vegas. I want to spend the next three days with my best friends, celebrating Arlo and Olivia and having fun.

Poppy glances at me from her middle seat. Julie, Caleb's wife, chose the aisle for easier access to the restroom because she's six months pregnant with their second child.

"What's going on?" Poppy whispers.

I glance up from the magazine I'd bought while waiting to board. "With what?"

Her eyes cut to those surrounding us, and she leans closer. "I noticed you slept at the apartment last night."

I adore Julie, and on the rare occasions that her parents or Caleb's aren't fighting for more time with their grandson, I babysit for them. But Poppy is like a sister to me and the only one I'm comfortable airing my current conflicting relationship status with, so I shake my head, returning my attention to the magazine.

Only a few seconds pass before Julie asks if Poppy's chosen a wedding date, which turns into conversations about venues, colors, flowers, and details that Poppy and I have been going over since her Christmas engagement. Only now, Poppy's enthusiasm is heightened, more animated. When Julie gets up to use the restroom, Poppy swings her green eyes to me, an attack visible in her narrowed glare.

I point at her before she can begin the barrage. "Turn your ring around and stop feeling guilty for being happy."

Her eyes widen, and she blinks.

"I'm not going to be mad at you for being happy. This isn't a jealousy game. Otherwise, our friendship would've ended years ago when I nearly failed Spanish, and you became the star student."

"It was the possessions that kept tripping you up," she says.

I shake my head. "It was Spanish that kept tripping me up. The point is, you're my best friend, and your happiness is important to me, and I don't ever want you to feel guilty for being happy."

"You're going through something right now. I don't want to make it harder."

"You won't. Things are a little weird right now, but that doesn't change you and me. Nothing changes us."

She leans closer. "Fine. I'll promise to stop filtering myself if you start telling me what's going on between you and Lincoln."

I glance across at the guys who are mid-conversation about cryptocurrencies, then to the restroom that Julie is leaving, and then to Poppy. "I don't know," I tell her honestly. "His neighbor was wearing his jersey the other day when she dropped off cookies for him and revealed he might be lying about where he was because Thursday when Pax was home, Lincoln was still at practice until nearly ten."

Julie slides into her seat before Poppy can reply, leaving her blinking through the confounding facts I've just dumped on her lap.

"Are you feeling okay, Julie?" I ask.

She grins. "I plan to mostly live vicariously through you both this weekend, so I hope you have a lot of fun and share the stories with me once we're flying back. My time is likely going to consist of the spa, extra naps, and all the buffets."

"I might join you for those naps and buffets," I tell her.

Across the aisle, Paxton laughs at something that's been said. I look from him to Lincoln, waiting for that simple moment when our eyes connect, and a dozen words are expressed without a single word, but his attention is on his phone.

Poppy glances from the guys to me, her concern and doubt apparent. My stomach coils, realizing this isn't simply in my own thoughts. She recognizes the discord as well, which somehow makes everything more real.

BY THE TIME WE LAND, my hope for having a fun and carefree weekend with friends is vying with a dozen other desires, none of which are appropriate or healthy. Ones that include making Lincoln jealous, or forgetting about him and spending the weekend on minimal sleep with excess alcohol to dim my anxiety, or confronting him and demanding he tells me the truth and get all the ugly accusations out on the table so we can start assigning blame.

Slot machines blink and shine, trying to lure us in, but we follow the crowds to the baggage claim, Lincoln and Paxton wearing baseball hats pulled low over their brows in an attempt to shade their faces because of all the places they could get recognized, it would likely be here in Vegas where bets are placed on teams.

Poppy takes my hand as though she can feel the energy pouring off me—maybe she can. Perhaps I'm that obvious. Lincoln glances back, his stare dropping to our entwined hands before cutting to my face for a half-second before facing forward again. Poppy's fingers constrict around mine. "He still cares," she whispers.

Flashbacks of sitting in my childhood bedroom, us demolishing a package of Oreos while we analyzed each look and word from Lincoln, create another ache in my chest.

Poppy squeezes tighter as I release a quiet sigh.

Men wearing black suits and holding small signs with our names printed across them are waiting in the baggage claim, and I instantly know who sent them.

Poppy and I exchange a look. She and Lincoln were both born into money, worlds where travel and personal chefs, and other luxuries that I didn't know existed—but Tyler Banks is another level of rich.

"This is going to be insane," Pax says before stopping in front of the men. "We just have to grab our bags, and we'll be ready," he tells one of the guys.

One of the men grins. "Your bags will be taken care of and brought to the hotel. Please come with us."

"That's all someone would have to say to me to abduct me," Poppy says wistfully.

A grin hits my face and grows when we step outside into the sunshine. It's chilly, but it feels like I haven't seen the sun since leaving Mexico. I turn my face toward it and close my eyes for a full second, appreciating my first full day off from everything.

Three black Mercedes wait outside, and the men open the back doors for us. Caleb and Julie climb into the first car, and Poppy and Pax go to the end. Lincoln adjusts his hat, then places his hand on my back, only it's too high to feel right because he marked his spot on me years ago. I slide into the car, Lincoln behind me. He closes the door before facing me.

"Is everything okay?"

I stare at him, my confidence waning, frustrating me further.

"Raegan," he says my name softly, concern pinching the skin between his brows.

Our driver gets into the driver's seat and welcomes us. Lincoln cuts his attention to him, a frown marring his brow as his jaw clenches.

"Welcome to Las Vegas," the driver says. "We'll have you to the Banks Resort in just a short moment. Do either of you need me to make any stops before we arrive?"

One of Lincoln's most consistent and predictable traits is his desire for privacy. He won't want to have this conversation with an audience.

"Did you give your jersey to a woman?"

His attention swings to me, his dark eyes blazing with questions. "What?"

"Did you give someone one of your jerseys?"

He shakes his head. "What?"

"It's a simple question."

"No."

"No?"

Frustration pinches his eyes. "What in the hell is going on? Why are you asking me this?"

I stare at him, my own anger rising to match his, but before I can respond, the car comes to a stop in front of the resort.

"This conversation isn't over," Lincoln grinds out, opening his door before the attendant can reach him.

The driver tries to meet my gaze, but I avoid him, pasting a smile on my face as I get out, hearing the squeals and excitement of greetings from my closest friends.

"Rae Rae!" Arlo calls my name from the sidewalk, and tears brim in my eyes as I look from him to Olivia, Chloe, Tyler, Nessie, Cooper, Rose, and Ian—the missing parts of our puzzle.

I push my purse higher on my shoulder and skirt around the front of the car, meeting Arlo in an embrace. A tear slips from my eye as he hugs me close.

We are an exchange of hugs and compliments, gentle laughter, and a few more tears being shed—mostly by me, but a few from Olivia as well. Chloe is the last person I hug, our arms remaining woven around each other's shoulders. Each of their moves hurt, but the extra year Nessie, Chloe, Ty, and Cooper spent in Seattle allowed us an additional year of memories and fun.

"Are you okay?" Chloe asks, her voice quiet.

I glance at her, hoping to lie, but tears battle my smile, winning the race. Before anyone notices, she turns, hugging me again. I swallow the lump in my throat, willing myself to gain control over my emotions and focus on one thing at a time, and right now, that is being here, present, celebrating Olivia and Arlo for three short days.

"Let's get this party started. You guys have to see these rooms. You're going to be ruined for all other hotels," Nessie says.

Chloe turns protectively, keeping her body between me and the rest to allow a small buffer to gain my composure. We head inside, excited chatter surrounding us as stories of our travel is shared. The air is sweet with the scents of vanilla and oranges, the latter further souring my mood.

Another man in a suit, this one heather gray, meets us, leading us to the elevators with a deck of hotel keys and cardstock folders with the hotel's emblem across the front in gold script.

He takes us to the elevators, dispersing the keys and packets to each couple along with his business card and the instructions to call him directly day or night if we have any questions or need anything, and assuring us that our bags would be waiting for us when we came back tonight.

"Bloody hell," Arlo says, trying his best to impersonate Tyler. "I can already tell it's going to be tough to leave." He wraps an arm around Olivia, exchanging a matching smile of adoration. "Let's go get this party started!"

11

LINCOLN

"One more," Rose says. "Move a little closer. Rae, I can only see your forehead."

We're posing for what feels like the hundredth photo of the afternoon, Rae on the opposite side of the group. Poppy notices me looking and gives me a hard stare. I don't have a fucking clue what is going on, but she clearly does.

"There's a cigar bar, and we need to celebrate this weekend with a quick visit," Ian says. "Ladies, would you like to join us?"

Poppy is the first to object, shaking her head. She looks at the others. "I'm going to head to the roller coaster if any of you want to join."

"I'll wait with you," Rae offers to Julie. The Robinson twins are the next to agree, Rose and Olivia opting to go with us.

Tyler peers around the casino like he's on the field, studying the lineup. "It's a busy weekend. Make sure you guys stay together. If you need anything, call." He gives Chloe a meaningful look.

"Did you see Rae's Instagram? She swam with literal sharks a month ago. We've got this." Vanessa says as she moves closer to Cooper and kisses him.

"Do you ever get confused when the twins are together?" Arlo asks as we part ways. It feels like a valid question because more than once today, I've found myself tripping over who was who, but admitting this makes me feel like a shitty friend.

Tyler raises a brow. "Confused?"

"Yeah, like, do you ever look over and check out your girlfriend and realize you're checking out her sister?" Arlo shakes his head. "I mean, they look identical. Knowing my luck, I'd probably end up kissing the wrong sister."

Olivia scoffs. "Here we go again with the luck."

Arlo's face splits with a smile as he hooks his arm around her waist. "I thought we settled this. When you're not around, I have bad luck, but I have the best of luck when you're with me. That's why I'm marrying you. Didn't you read our prenup? You aren't allowed to be more than a hundred feet away from me at any given time. I assumed that's why you said yes to cigars."

She rolls her eyes in response.

Arlo pulls her closer. "I'm your ball and chain, babe."

Cooper, who has always been good-natured and easy-going, grins. "Chloe would punch me before letting me kiss her, and Vanessa would do the same to Tyler."

"So you do get them confused," Arlo says like a confirmation.

Coop looks at Tyler, and they both shake their head. "No," Tyler voices. "They look similar, but after a while, they look very different."

"I'm a perceptive female, and I get them confused once in a while," Rose interjects.

Arlo gives her a high five. "Truth bomb."

"Their personalities are very different, and so are their mannerisms. You'll also notice little details that add up to significant differences in the way they stand, their expressions, their eyes, their mouths, even their voices are different," Tyler says.

"I think that's kind of beautiful," Olivia says. "So often, people assume you fall in love with someone because of what they look like, but this scenario proves who we are on the inside truly matters. Maybe our hearts have eyes too."

Pax looks at me. "They must because my sister fell for this asshat." A chorus of laughter greets his words.

"Did you ever have a thing for Rae?" Arlo asks, turning to Caleb.

Caleb shakes his head. "That relationship has been strictly platonic since day one. She's like my sister."

"Yeah, I can see that. I never got that suppressed 'I want to rip your clothes off' vibe between the two of you," Rose says.

"Thank fuck," I say.

Tyler glances at me, sympathy in his eyes as he grins.

Arlo flat-out laughs. "When are you planning to propose to Rae Rae? My money was on you being the first one to pop the question. Or do you still have some lasting commitment phobias?"

My stomach falls, and embarrassment and pride battle in my gut. I don't know if I prefer they assume I haven't asked or know the truth.

"That hesitation points to phobia," Pax says with a chuckle. More laughter, this one makes me wish for a drink as it grates against my sanity.

"We can't give Lincoln the full weight of this prize. Rae has her own bag of relationship phobias," Caleb says, pulling the ground out from under me again. "Do you remember her reaction when I told her I was proposing to Julie?" He looks at Pax and gives a halfhearted shrug.

Pax shakes his head, a dark look passing over his features that dissipates as we continue walking. "Our dad definitely left a mark. That entire situation was...." He shakes his head again as his words trail off. His thoughts are likely traveling back to the night their dad's girlfriend tried to hurt Rae while mine travel back a bit further, to the weeks before we learned about the affair when Rae was carrying the entirety of their secret, back to the night I dropped her off at her house after my dad and Carol's engagement party. She looked at me with those soulful eyes and told me I was right, and nothing lasts forever. It's a memory I'd completely forgotten, likely because I thought it was a load of shit then—and still do.

"They don't have to be married to be committed," Rose interjects.

"Commitment is so much bigger than marriage, just like love is so much more than just a feeling."

"I'll help you out of the hot seat," Tyler says. "Be sure to all have your passports by next year."

"What?" Arlo asks, turning his attention.

Tyler smiles proudly and nods. "I've been planning a proposal for months, so Chloe doesn't expect it. Don't any of you say anything."

We all look at Arlo, even Olivia.

"What?" he asks. "Good relationships aren't built on a foundation of secrets." He makes eye contact with me. Arlo has been known for letting things slip in the past, but it's always been things that are either inconsequential or things that needed to be said, like when Paxton began dating Candace, and everyone knew she was trouble and drama, Arlo was the first to admit it aloud. He can keep secrets—the ones that matter—better than most.

We step into the cigar shop, another opulent space. Shelves are stacked with boxes of cigars from around the world, and a bar runs along the far wall. It's early, and only a few people are inside.

Our group enters like smoke, spreading around the room, looking through the different bottles of alcohol and cigars. "I had no idea there were so many different kinds of cigars," Olivia tells Rose as the two head toward a shelf.

Arlo stops beside me, reaching for a single cigar that he holds to his nose. "This is pretty great, right? Who would have imagined eight years ago when we all met that this is where we'd be?"

"You mean that we're still hanging out with Paxton?" I ask.

He laughs so hard he places a hand on his stomach. "Too bad he wasn't closer to hear that one."

A brand of cigar slows my thoughts. It's the same kind my dad gifted me for graduating high school, again when I was drafted, and a third when I graduated from Brighton. "I'm glad you waited until the off-season so we could be here to celebrate with you guys."

"You guys are my family. Distance doesn't change that."

I nod. "Are you guys planning to spend some time in Washington this summer?"

"Yeah. After the honeymoon, we'll be there. We've been trying to decide what to do with housing. I like Coach, but living under his roof is a little weird. I still worry he might greet me with a shotgun one morning, which keeps my hands strictly out of the endzones at all times."

"Nah, Coach is more methodical. He'd go for your weak spot, try breaking your knee, and make it look like an accident."

Arlo laughs. "You're so right." He grabs another cigar and smells it. "What's going on with you and Rae Rae?" he asks, voice dropped, his tone serious.

I cut my attention to him.

Sympathy stares back at me. "You made some serious eye contact back there with me," he says. "Go ahead, spill it. I'm ready."

"It's nothing."

"Oh, there's definitely something."

I stare at the piles of cigars for a moment and then release a sigh. "I asked Rae to marry me."

Arlo drops the cigar and doesn't make a move to pick it up. "And...?"

"She said no."

He winces. "Shit, man. I'm sorry." He shakes his head. "Did she say why?"

"It was my fault. We'd been to dinner with my dad, and it was a shit show, and when we got back, I just blurted out the question. There was no ring or speech or anything."

Arlo shakes his head. "Pres, this is Rae we're talking about. She's probably the last person to care about a big ass fancy ring."

"Are you saying it was just me she was rejecting?"

He shakes his head again. "No. Don't go getting insecure. You know better than that. Rae looks at you like you hung the fucking stars."

"So, if it wasn't me, and it wasn't the ring, then why?" I shake my head.

"My guess, knowing Rae, she was worried about you. She might be a little scared, too. Caleb isn't wrong. Their dad really fucked things up. You remember our junior year when that shit went down. She was pretty distant for a while. But, if I were a betting man— which I am—" He grins, but it fades too quickly. "She knows your relationship with your dad and how you were the eternal bachelor before the two of you began dating. Hell, it took you most of a year of not dating before you started dating."

"We've been together for five years," I object. "We picked out furniture together. Her shampoo's in my shower, we have designated sections in the closet, and the remote lives on her nightstand. I haven't been the eternal bachelor since I met her."

"Maybe she needs to hear that. We all got drafted and had to move or make plans to see each other, forcing us to show our hands. I wasn't about to live on the opposite side of the country as Liv, so I went to dinner with Coach and told him that I loved his daughter and requested his approval to ask her to move with me. Then, I had to convince Liv, which was scary as fucking shit. No one wants to feel vulnerable and weak, yet there I was, basically professing that I wasn't going to be able to live or breathe or play football unless she came with me, knowing that I was asking her to sacrifice a ton—her family, you guys, and it was another huge move where she knew no one to an even colder climate." He lifts one shoulder with a shrug. "Maybe Rae just needs a reminder that you would want to hang those stars for her."

"Arlo," Olivia calls. "There's a cigar named after me."

Arlo claps a hand to my shoulder, his expression turning serious again. "Are you going to let one night, one question, one conversation fuck things up between the two of you?" He waits for half a beat and then continues, "Do you remember when I was all bent out of shape about Liv and her ex, and you told me to swallow my pride and talk to her, and that shit is rarely as bad as it seems?" He raises one eyebrow, not giving me a chance to respond before saying, "Time to show up, President." He pats me and then wanders in the direction of Olivia.

12

RAEGAN

We travel the Strip like tourists, our pace slow, stopping every few feet, and obliging whenever someone suggests we take a picture.

"How's school going?" I ask Chloe as we step outside, a breeze making me shudder. Poppy, who is on my other side, huddles closer to me.

"There are days I want to cry," Chloe admits before releasing a quiet laugh. "In some ways, I just wish it were over."

"Yeah, right," Nessie says. "I'm convinced you're going to get three doctorates, so you never have to leave school."

Chloe gives a chaste smile. "How are things going with your master's degree?"

"Exhausting," I admit. "There are days when I seriously wish I could turn back the hands of time and go back to when we were all at Brighton, back when I had time to hang out and sleep and drink a full cup of coffee in one sitting."

"I miss Brighton, too," Nessie says. "I miss the parties and our Friendsgivings."

"I miss our Friendsivings, too," Poppy says. "And the bonfires and the consistency of things."

"Do you miss college?" I ask, looking at Julie.

She looks at me, a thoughtful expression that has her brows inching up. "Sometimes, but I wouldn't want to go back. Those years were fun, but so is now. I'm married to my best friend. I have the coolest two-year-old in the world, and if I want to have pancakes for dinner, I have pancakes for dinner. If I want to paint my bathroom sherbet orange, I paint my bathroom sherbet orange." She shrugs.

"Yeah, but adulting comes with bills, and taxes, and jobs, and dishes," Nessie says. "So many dishes. And laundry."

Julie scrunches her nose. "I feel you on this. I feel like I'm doing laundry twice a day, but although college was fun, it was stressful at the time, too. Remember caring about what we wore and how we looked every day? And all the drama and rumors? Now, I don't give a single fuck what someone thinks about me. I go to the grocery store in my sweatpants. And if someone in my life is toxic, I now have the confidence and self-awareness to recognize that and not waste time and energy on those relationships. And can we talk about the benefits of having our own homes? Don't get me wrong, I loved seeing you guys all the time, but there is something pretty great about having sex whenever and wherever I want. I mean, I have so many urges right now with all these baby hormones, and it's pretty great to act on them and whenever I want to ... assuming our little one isn't around, of course."

We collectively laugh.

"House shopping has been really fun," Poppy admits.

Julie nods. "Wait until you start decorating your house, and wedding planning will be great, and getting married, and planning your family. I'm grateful for my time at Brighton, but I wouldn't trade now for any amount of money." Confidence shines in her eyes.

Chloe purses her lips. "I feel like you've just hit me with a truth bomb. I mean, I get to live in England, travel to foreign countries and stay in beautiful hotels, and wake up to chocolate pastries and Tyler's head between my legs. I miss you guys so damn much, but things are pretty perfect when I think about it."

Nessie nods. "I love working with Coop, and traveling between Florida and England, and making our own rules."

"Thanks for not mentioning sex," Chloe says, making the rest of us laugh.

"I only did it for you, but since you mentioned Tyler's head between your legs, I think it's worth mentioning that naked days are well worth the price of taxes."

Poppy's grip on my arm tightens, a silent sign of her support.

Chloe looks at her watch. "Maybe we should come back and do the roller coaster tomorrow? We have the VIP room at the club rented. We should probably head back so we can change and get ready."

I turn around, trying to recall which direction we came from, prepared to walk back to the hotel, but Chloe is already calling someone and requesting rides.

Moments later, similar cars to those that picked us up from the airport arrive. Jokes about the night are shared, the mood light as we travel the short distance back to the hotel.

"Want to get ready together?" Poppy asks as we step off the elevator.

The truth is, I'd like to be alone, but that will likely only deepen my funk, so I try pasting on a smile and nod.

"Want to get ready in my room or yours?" she asks.

"Yours, let me just grab my makeup bag and a dress."

Poppy follows me to my door, likely sensing my mood better than me. "Wow," she says, following me through the door into a living room with three couches that surround a fireplace with an expansive TV. On either side of the fireplace are floor-to-ceiling windows that look out onto the strip. Beyond the living room is a bedroom with French doors, a king-size bed with an upholstered headboard visible along the far wall.

"This is insane," I say, still peering around at all the details. "This place is as big as Lincoln's condo." There are few places I've seen that compare to Lincoln's father's house, which not only is grand and massive but also sits on a piece of Seattle real estate that is likely worth more than the house itself. But my recent trip to Mexico had me sleeping in a sleeping bag on a twin bed that was only two feet away from my roommate. This place feels like a mansion in comparison.

"There's a gift," Poppy says, approaching the coffee table.

"Open it," I tell her.

"I'm trying to prove to myself that I have boundaries."

"Boundaries? What are those?"

Poppy laughs outright. "It's your room. You should open it."

I walk closer, peering at the large gold box with a card sitting atop. I lift the square lid to find a tray of truffles, a bottle of Lincoln's favorite bourbon, and two Tiffany-blue tees with #TeamArlivia printed across the front.

"Arlivia," Poppy reads aloud for the third time, laughing even harder. I hold one up and realize there's more print on the back.

"Kostas, family rule: Blood is thicker, but choice is stronger."

We head into the bedroom, finding Lincoln's and my suitcases beside a door that I open to reveal a spacious closet.

"Rae, you have to see the bathroom!" Poppy calls from ahead of me. "It's so pretty."

Poppy's taking pictures of the large soaking tub as I step inside.

"Look at this shower," she says. "It's huge."

I love Lincoln's condo, and the views from it are incredible, but the bathroom has always seemed like a forgotten space, built before people cared about soaking tubs or the luxury of large showers and dual showerheads. This shower spans nearly the length of the wall, a wall that looks like river rock, and the floor is dark honeycomb-shaped tiles that slant toward a nearly invisible drain at the edge of the shower, all enclosed by large panels of glass.

"Three days isn't going to be long enough," Poppy says, moving to the counter where she rifles through a tray of amenities. "This might be the first time I use hotel shampoo."

"You don't use hotel shampoo?" I ask.

"You do?"

I shrug. "I didn't know I wasn't supposed to."

Poppy grins. "This stuff you should use."

I think back to the last time I was in a hotel this nice. Last summer, I was in the midst of my master's, keeping us in Seattle, but the year before that, Lincoln had booked us a trip to St. Lucia to celebrate my graduating with my dual bachelor's degrees. Our hotel room had entire open walls that looked out upon the ocean without the obstruction of glass or even curtains and a small infinity pool that stretched to the very edge.

"Are you okay?" Poppy asks concern bringing her several steps closer.

I nod, though my thoughts are in disagreement. "I keep thinking about what everyone was saying about how their lives have improved and that this is a better chapter, and all I can think is how much I want to go back. I don't know that I love this anymore."

"Love what?"

"School. Cetology. Getting my master's."

Poppy stares at me, and the gentle smile on her lips encourages me to continue. "I mean, I love the idea of it, I love the possibility, but I don't love that I don't see anyone anymore. I don't love that Lincoln's so busy and that our schedules are forever colliding. I don't love that I'm in debt up to my eyeballs with student loans, and I'm working so few hours that I can barely afford rent." I release a heavy sigh. "I'm scared that I'm chasing a dream job at the cost of having a life. I compare now and our first couple of years in college, and I would go back in a heartbeat if I could." Tears blur my vision. "And that girl who baked Lincoln cookies and delivered them while wearing his jersey had given him a stupid orange, and I'm irrationally angry about a stupid piece of fruit. And I'm so mad and sad and worried that I can't see straight."

Poppy walks closer, not stopping until her arms are tied behind my shoulders, hugging me. She doesn't say a word, but she doesn't have to. Her presence and comfort are enough as my heart feels the slightest hint of relief with my admission.

"I'm instilling some new rules," Poppy says once my tears have settled and my breaths have slowed.

I take a step back, wiping at my cheeks.

"Rule one, we have breakfast together every Saturday, just the two of us. We have to make sure we're talking about things and checking in. Rule two, we seek out retribution together, and by this, I mean that cookie-baking wannabe homewrecker is going down. Three, you have to let me know when you've been maimed. I can't help you patch the ship if you don't let me know you're sinking. You're so stubborn and strong, and sometimes it's hard to know if something is wrong because you put on such a tough face. But you don't have to do that, Rae. I don't want you to do that. Regardless of boys, work, goals, or anything else, we're a team—always have been, always will be." She gives me a long stare. "And rule four, this is a biggie, we watch TV and catch up on our shows on Thursdays because Paxton talks through *every* show, predicting what's going to happen next, and it drives me up the wall."

I snigger. "He always has."

Poppy places her hand on my shoulder, her face still somber. "Regarding the rest, I think we should go and have fun tonight. Not worry about school or work or anything else besides having a good time. Then we do it again tomorrow and Monday. Then, Tuesday, on our flight home, we can make plans to get everything sorted. But for now, I think detaching and having fun will help a lot."

I nod, wiping the last of my stray tears away, clinging to conviction like a lifeline.

With my makeup, a dress I almost didn't pack, and shoes I probably shouldn't have packed, we head down the hall to Poppy's room.

While I plug in a curling iron, she discreetly texts someone.

"Rule five," I say, turning around to face her. "No concealing happiness. I want you to flaunt that shit."

"I appreciate that, and I will, but a little discretion while you work through things seems like a very appropriate amendment to rule five."

"I hate feeling this sense of insecurity," I admit. "I hate wondering if something happened while I was gone, and in that same vein, it seems almost callous and ignorant to imagine something couldn't have happened. I mean, he's Lincoln—gorgeous, successful, smart...." I lick my lips that have turned dry, finding it easier to list off the common descriptions that would be found on an internet search for eligible bachelors rather than the personal traits that have had me falling for him time and time again for the past seven years —two more than we've been dating—like his deep sense of loyalty, how he builds others up whether on the football field or me in a parking lot grieving my sister leaving. It's how he's always aware of others, reading their emotions and intentions and then assisting in any way he can, sometimes in the most subtle of ways and other times more obvious. It's the way I can be in a room filled with people and still feel his presence because there's something about him that speaks to me on a level so much greater than I'll ever be able to comprehend.

"It's okay to feel that way. We all go through that sometimes, and it's scary. I think it's because you're missing that point where you reconnect. You need his assurance, and that doesn't make you weak or needy. It just means you're human."

"I need a drink."

Poppy grins. "Good, because drinks, fun, and zero regrets are what's on the menu tonight."

"Where's Pax and the others?" I ask, applying a final coat of mascara.

Poppy sets her phone down and slips on a black heel. Her dress is black, with sheer stripes that cover her torso, arms, and upper chest.

"You look like a knockout," I tell her again. Poppy is easily our most fashionable friend, a cross between classy and modern that always impresses me.

She smiles nervously. "Is it too see-through?"

I shake my head. "No. Not at all." I tug at the top of my dress, which is rose gold and covered in sequins that change in color to make the dress ombre, darkening at my thighs.

"Olivia and Rose are getting ready, but Pax and Lincoln went to the bar to have a drink."

I forget about my dress and ensuring my strapless bra isn't showing. "Pax isn't meddling, is he? I don't want him trying to strongarm or influence Lincoln."

Poppy shakes her head. "I haven't told him anything. He said Lincoln asked him."

Nerves fire through my body, my insecurities growing. I've always wondered what would happen if things went awry between Lincoln and me. Specifically, I've always questioned if he'd tell Pax first in an attempt to salvage their friendship.

"You look like you need that drink," Poppy says.

"Are the others going with us?"

"We'll meet them there. Let's go."

We set off down the hall, Poppy complimenting the gold heels I'm wearing. They're one of three pairs that I own because, between work and school, I live in tennis shoes.

"Do you mind if we walk?" I ask her as the elevator doors open to the lobby.

"Not at all." She reaches for my hand, threading our fingers.

There's something great about Vegas and the infinite styles, moods, and trends. We pass people wearing tracksuits and others in tuxes, some in shorts, jeans, ball gowns, and everything in between, showing the multitude of reasons this city has drawn people here.

"I think we need to go down a level," Poppy says, sliding her phone into her purse and pointing at a sign for an elevator.

"Oh, it smells like urine." I cough, and Poppy gags as we step into the small elevator car.

"Maybe there's another way down," she starts to say, but before we can move, a man appears in the elevator, naked except for a tall pair of socks and tennis shoes. He hits the button for the doors to close.

"No," Poppy blurts, shaking her head. "No way. You can't ride in here with us. Where are your clothes?"

The naked man turns to face us, a hand discretionally placed in an attempt to cover himself as the doors fall shut. He grins, cheeks red, eyes dilated. "Do you guys happen to have directions to your hotel room? I think I lost my clothes there."

I'm trying to focus on the situation and an appropriate response for this incredibly inappropriate moment, but I can't stop staring at the mass of dark pubic hair poking out from around his hand. His legs are toothpicks, and his upper body resembles a barrel.

"I'll give you twenty bucks to take a picture with me," he says, his words slurred.

"How? You aren't wearing any pants," Poppy points out his lack of a wallet.

The guy moves, reaching for his socks, revealing himself.

We shriek in unison, and he jumps, startled from our reaction or too drunk to recognize it's because of him because he turns around like there's something behind him that has earned our reaction.

The doors open, and a couple is on the other side, looking from naked guy to us attempting to shield our eyes, back to naked guy.

"What the fuck, dude?" the guy asks. "What in the hell's wrong with you? Where are your pants?"

"Where's his penis?" the woman asks. "Someone's going to get lost in that forest, hunting for a little nut."

"It's cold," naked guy objects. "In the sunshine, he's like a palm tree." Rejection or sense seems to kick in enough that naked guy steps off the elevator and starts walking.

We share a laugh with the couple before heading in the opposite direction. "He was smaller than my thumb," I say, sticking my thumb up. "I didn't even know that was possible."

"I didn't even see it at first," Poppy admits with a laugh. "My eyes feel violated. I can't believe I asked him for his wallet. That question was a hundred-percent reflex."

"You mean you didn't subconsciously want to see what he was hiding behind the curtain?"

Poppy makes a sound that is between a scoff and a gag. "I definitely wasn't expecting a finger puppet show."

Laughter has me gripping my stomach.

13

LINCOLN

I pull my hat down a little lower as I sit back down from signing another autograph. It's a strange feeling being recognized, one I hope I never get used to.

"How has house shopping been going?" I ask Paxton. We went through two casinos after going to the cigar bar, showing Caleb around since this is his first trip to Sin City. With Tyler's commentary, it felt like my first time as well. When we made it back to the hotel, I suggested to Pax that we have a drink with the vague excuse that the girls were still getting ready. In reality, guilt was beginning to gnaw at my conscience. Raegan is as independent as they come, but I know Pax has felt a greater responsibility since their dad took things from bad to worse and then made little attempt to resolve the shitstorm from which he slunk.

Pax lifts the glass of Coke he'd ordered and takes a pull. "We found this property that is fucking amazing. It's big enough for us to build on and still have a ton of privacy. It's forty acres, surrounded with woods, and still convenient to downtown, so it won't add extra time commuting."

"Forty acres? Shit."

He nods. "The sticker price gave me a mild heart attack, but it gives us so many things that we both want. The privacy, the chance for her dad to design and build the house how Poppy wants, a huge yard, a greenhouse, a pool, and place for a chicken coop."

"A chicken coop?"

Pax nods, taking another drink. "She wants to raise chickens and adopt other farm animals.

This has me laughing. I can imagine finding Raegan at their house, her and Poppy sitting among a dozen chickens and cows, reading books, and caring for them. "We're going to be replaced by those farm animals, you know?"

"Yup," he says, taking another drink. "We're going to have to up our game. I was looking at getting a condo in the city for when the house is being built, a place we could keep afterward so I can drag her away on occasion."

"So, it's happening? You found *the* place?"

"We put in an offer Thursday night," he says. "We're waiting to hear back from our realtor." A heavy and hopeful sigh leaves him as he grips the mostly empty glass. "Since the girls' lease is up next month, the timing works out pretty well. It's not like either of them stay at their apartment, anyway." He looks at me, his easygoing nature replaced with intent. "What about you and Rae? Is she planning to move into your condo, or are you guys thinking about finding a new place together?"

Admitting that we haven't discussed this seemingly simple step, one that most would likely be perceived as our next natural step, has me taking a drink of my bourbon. "Things have been so crazy lately that we haven't finalized plans."

"God damn, I wish I still drank," he says, running a hand through his hair. "You're my best friend, and it's almost normal to me now that you're dating my little sister, but I won't lie and tell you I don't worry about it sometimes. On the one hand, I feel like I should be asking you what your intentions are and making sure you're keeping your focus on her and her best interests, and on the other hand, I want to be your friend and not pressure you into doing anything. I'm in a lose-lose situation."

I kick out my foot. "You know my intentions."

He stares at me and slowly shakes his head. "I don't think I do." He raises his eyebrows fractionally. "I do know that something's off. You've been acting weird since Christmas."

I take another drink, staring at him, waiting for him to call out my cowardice. But Pax just sips his drink and waits.

"I found out my dad's getting a divorce and that I have a little brother who's two that I never knew about, and then later that same night, I asked your sister to marry me, and she said no."

Paxton stares at me as I repeat the story for the second time in a matter of hours, his eyes rounding as each part of my sentence hits him with a new level of surprise and shock. "Fuck," he says, looking for the waitress, and motioning to get me a refill. "Where do I even start?" He runs his hand down his face. "She said no?" Disbelief coats his voice. "You were clear, right?"

"As oppposed to what?"

"Like you didn't say something stupid like why don't you change your last name or something ridiculous."

"Is your drink spiked? Who says shit like that?"

He sputters. "I don't know, but she wouldn't have said no." He shakes his head. "There's no way."

"I fucked it up. I asked her in the goddamn parking garage without a ring or a plan after walking out on my dad and surprise new family, and then she got called to Mexico before we could work through it all, and shit has just been weird since."

Pax blows out a breath. Clearly, whatever Poppy knows, she hasn't told him. "Want me to talk to her?"

I shake my head. "No. I'm only telling you this because I feel like I owe you this out of respect because you're my best friend and because you and Rae are so close. Not that she's one for tradition, but I kind of feel like I should have come to you beforehand to make sure you were okay with it all."

"You two always have taken the hardest path." Pax shakes his head and finishes his drink. "Take your own advice, Beckett. If she's still the person who makes you feel like you can breathe and gives sense to life, then tell her. You can't let this stop you."

"I know," I tell him.

He glances at his phone when it vibrates with a message. "Shit. We should go. Poppy said they just had a naked guy in the elevator with them."

"Here?" I stand, twisting to find the elevators.

"No, they're at the club," he says, punching letters on his screen. "They're laughing about it." He shakes his head. "I have to change. Tyler said we have to wear a damn jacket."

I'm restless and irritable as we take the elevator up to our rooms. Inside, I find our suitcases, Rae's still propped open. I pull on jeans, a collared button-down, and a jacket before shoving my feet into a pair of dress shoes.

I send Pax a message that I'll meet him there and slide my wallet and phone into my pockets. My strides are long, purposeful as I make my way to the lobby.

"Hey," Tyler calls, catching my attention from where he's next to a man in a suit, who he gives a few more words, then steps away. "You want to ride with me to the club?"

I nod, following him outside where a black car is waiting.

It's strange to sit in the back of a car, and it's even stranger to sit in the back of a car beside another dude. "Cozy," I say.

He chuckles. "Brings me back to days at Brighton and riding on the damn bus."

"Do you miss it?" I ask.

"Brighton?"

I shake my head. "Football."

Tyler tips his chin upward. "More than I expected, but I'm also happier than I deserve or predicted, and it has nothing to do with work or football."

The car slides to a stop, and the driver starts to step out before Tyler stops him with a quick assurance. We step out of the car, the night air greeting us with a cold snap. I follow Tyler inside, avoiding the gazes of a pair of girls who look to catch our attention.

Walking with Tyler is like carrying a personal VIP pass. We skip to the front of the line and are instantly given lime green bracelets and an escort to show us inside. There are guys on the team who like to party like this. "This surprises me," I admit. "I didn't picture you as the clubbing type."

Tyler looks at me. "I'm expected to do this kind of shit. I'm not surprised you aren't the clubbing type."

I grin. "Maybe if it didn't involve other people, I'd like it more."

He cracks a smile. We share a mutual aversion to bullshit and people. I prefer my circle to be small, free from rumors and drama, which is why this snafu with Rae has been eating at me. We haven't had drama between us in years, sticking to a policy of honesty and openness.

Tyler and I are led up a set of stairs to a private lounge that looks out across the club, and before I can finish looking around, Tyler's tipping the woman and ordering us a round of drinks. He walks to a spot and holds the rail, grinning as he looks across the throngs of people. He stops and points. I step closer, looking in the direction he's referencing, and see Rae laughing at something Poppy is saying to her.

"Hey," Paxton calls from behind us. Ian, Arlo, Cooper, and another host join us in the private room. The host acknowledges Tyler before disappearing downstairs. "Let's all move to Vegas and do this every weekend," Pax says, looking across the crowds and strobe lights.

"They let you in while wearing those?" I ask, spotting Paxton wearing the same damn pair of shorts we'd procured for him years ago after he lost a game of strip poker.

"Let me? They fucking rolled out the red carpet for me," Pax says. "Who's ready to start house shopping?"

"You're sure about that?" Tyler asks, motioning to where the girls are dancing, men joining them in droves.

"Fuck me," Pax mutters.

It's déjà vu, watching from here, recalling when Raegan started at Brighton with us. Paxton had tried issuing a warning to keep guys away from both Rae and Poppy, one that few listened to. More than once, I stepped in, trying to convince myself it was for his benefit when really it was my own sanity I was trying to salvage as I cock blocked other guys.

"I ordered a round of shots. Let's have a toast, and then we can go tell them all to bugger off," Tyler says, motioning to the table where a waiter is setting shot glasses.

Cooper groans and then laughs. "You son of a bitch."

Tyler laughs.

"I'm missing the punchline," Ian admits looking between them.

Cooper passes him a shot. "Have a slippery nipple," he says.

Tyler laughs harder.

"It's a long story," Cooper says, shaking his head and reaching for a second glass that he raises. "To Arlo."

We each grab a shot, Paxton's filled with Coke. "To Arlo," we say in unison and tip our glasses back. It's smooth and overly sweet, leaving a cherry in my mouth.

We take the stairs down to the darkened club, the lights overhead turning the same shade of green as our bracelets as a new song plays. The club is packed, splintering us as we head in the direction of the girls.

Eventually, I spot Rose, who's clearly trying to lose the attention of a guy who's not accepting her rebuff. I bump into the guy with my shoulder and then step in front of him, my anger channeling to a worthy target. "She told you to get lost," I tell him.

The guy looks from me to Rose, back to me as though trying to determine who would win if this came down to a fight.

Arlo appears at my side. "Think again, asshole. That's my future wifey's best friend, and this here's my brother. We're like fucking hyenas, you mess with one of us, and you get the entire damn clan."

The guy takes a step back with a quick shake of his head before moving into the crowd.

"That guy was up all of our asses," Rose says. "It's a shame you guys weren't here thirty minutes ago. I thought Nessie was going to punch him."

I glance around, trying to find Rae.

"Rae just went to the restroom with Poppy and Chloe. We're going in groups of three because it's so busy," Rose explains.

I nod, a note of relief hitting me that the girls are smart before aggression hits me for them having to go in pairs or more to ensure their safety in the first place.

It's only seconds before they appear, and I realize Chloe likely accompanied them because Rae and Poppy are both glassy-eyed and giggling, revealing they've had too much to drink.

Pax scoffs. "At this rate, we're going to have to carry them back to the hotel."

Rose laughs. "You're not wrong, but this is what we're here for. Zero regrets." She calls out a cheer and then heads for Olivia.

Poppy spots us, her arm linked with Rae's. She steers them toward us. Rae stops when she notices Paxton's shorts, shaking her head in protest.

"No! Why?" she yells, cringing as she turns her attention away from him.

Pax has a shit-eating grin as he places both hands on his hips.

"I've already been scarred tonight," Rae says, shaking her head.

"We saw a penis," Poppy adds, laughing so hard her shoulders curl. "It was so tiny." She giggles again and lifts her thumb. "*So* tiny. I mean, relationships are clearly so much more than sex, but can I just say how glad I am that you'd need both hands to cover yourself?"

Rae cringes. "Friendship rule eight. We don't talk about my brother's junk."

"I thought we were on rule seven?" Poppy asks.

"It can be rule seven and eight," Rae says.

Pax exchanges a look with me, a silent look of confirmation that takes me back to the same page of memories that I'd been reliving upstairs, back to when Pax would call upon us to watch out for the two of them. Only, tonight, it annoys me because this has been my role for five years, one I don't need to be reminded of because there's nothing I take as seriously as Rae's safety.

"We have to go upstairs for a little while," Nessie says, wrapping an arm around Raegan's neck. Jealousy used to stab me when a guy noticed Rae. Now it hits with a vengeance as Rae acknowledges her friend when she still hasn't looked toward me.

"Upstairs?" Rae asks.

"There's a private room," Nessie tells her.

"You had me at a place to sit down," Rae says, weaving her arm around Nessie's shoulders as Poppy slips free and moves to stand by Pax.

Nessie points. "To the private room."

Coop redirects her hand in the opposite direction to where the room is. "This is why you can't go hiking without GPS," he says.

She grins. Clearly, she's had a few drinks as well. We head toward the private room, guys periodically moving when they catch sight of them, and then stepping out of the way when they notice Coop and I a step behind.

In the private room, we find chairs spread in a large circle.

Ian stops behind me, eyebrows raised in question.

"We aren't playing truth or dare, are we?" Tyler asks. "Because I hate that game."

Rose grins. "So much better." She rubs her hands. "Everyone, take a seat."

"Rose..." Poppy says though she's looking at Rae.

"You didn't...." Rae adds, turning from Poppy to Rose.

"Oh, I did." She says.

Rae bites her bottom lip, looking back at Poppy. "I need another drink." She turns behind her and winces at the sight of Paxton. "You're giving me nightmares."

"You and your boyfriend are who gave me these shorts," he reminds her.

"I'm still regretting it," she fires back.

Olivia grins and takes Rae's arm, leading her to a seat as the rest of us fill the remaining chairs.

"What's going on?" Olivia asks, looking around to see who's willing to confess the answer.

Rose clears her throat. "As the matron of honor, I decided we all needed to enjoy one last crazy night before our best friends become hitched and never see another set of breasts or penis again."

Music starts, and the door opens. A guy dressed as a firefighter and another dressed as a police officer step in, followed by a woman dressed as a doctor and another as a nurse.

My attention swings to Rae, who looks at me then, her expression surprisingly sober from her seat across from me. I try to read her eyes that watch me with a sense of expectation that leaves me restless and confused.

Rose passes stacks of bills around as objections are met with shocked expressions.

"I consider myself pretty secure," Chloe says. "But can we not test my jealousy boundaries?" She looks at Tyler, who lifts both palms.

"Your breasts are the only set I care to see," he tells her.

"Rose," Olivia says. "Maybe we should call this off."

"Yeah, we already saw a rando's penis," Poppy chimes in, standing from her seat next to Rae. "We don't need a second show."

The fireman approaches her like a mark, grinding against her. Poppy's eyes widen with shock, and the first laugh breaks the room's tension coming from Vanessa.

"It's just for fun," Rose says. "There's no touching the talent."

The woman outfitted as a doctor stops in front of me, releasing a button on her shirt and then another. Across from me, I feel Rae's stare. Her face is stoic, not giving a hint as to what she's truly thinking or silently willing me to understand. I'm not the only one who notices since the next thing I see is the firefighter dropping his pants and straddling her lap.

Rae shakes her head, then wipes at her cheek and moves to stand. The guy grabs her hands, moving closer, rubbing against her chest.

I'm out of my chair in a second, nearly knocking the stripper in front of me over. Pax has to shoot out an arm to ensure she doesn't fall. The money Rose had given me scatters across the ground like leaves in October.

I move behind the male stripper, my hands balled into fists, trying to collect myself and remember they're being paid to do this at someone else's request. "Hands off," I say.

He turns, looking over his shoulder, both hands raised. "Just doing my job," he says.

I reach for my wallet, tearing it open and pulling out a stack of bills that I shove at him. "You're done."

He looks at the cash, then takes it before looking back at Rae. "You didn't pay me," he says.

"Fucking hell," Tyler says.

Something falls, and then a hand clasps around my wrist. Ian's at my side, his grip a firm warning, his chair upturned. "My buddy might kill you if you don't move," Ian warns the guy. "So, you might reconsider his offer."

I take a step closer. "Move, asshole. She's mine."

Rae scoots her chair back far enough that she's clear of the stripper and stands. With tears in her eyes and conviction on her face, she says, "I am yours. I've always been yours, so why aren't you mine?"

14

RAEGAN

The room falls eerily still. Everyone is silent. Even the music in the club seems to dim. If I weren't feeling so emotionally charged, I'd probably be embarrassed.

Lincoln stares at me, jealousy and annoyance have him clenching his jaw, but hurt and betrayal are present in his eyes that are pinned on me.

"You lied to me," I say, disregarding where we are as emotions and built-up tension take over. "You told me you were at practice late, but you weren't." I shake my head, recalling this is only a piece of the mistrust.

His brows dip with confusion, but before he can refute the fact, I move closer to the stripper dressed as a nurse, hand her the stack of money, and move for the stairs. Lincoln moves behind me, and I stop to face him. "I need a moment."

"We need to talk."

Instinctively, I shake my head. "Not right now."

"Rae—"

"Respect me enough to give me this," I say, swiping at the tears that slip from my eyes. "You've requested space, and I gave it to you. This is me, asking you to return that favor."

He stops like a glass wall has been erected.

Poppy begins to move, but she's more of a lightweight than I am, and she sways, causing her to grab the chair Arlo's sitting in.

"I'm sober," Chloe says, standing from her seat. "I'll come with you."

"Chloe," Tyler says, offering something to her as she passes.

I take the stairs, regretting my heels as my feet ache with each step, embarrassment catching up to me like the scent of smoke after a bonfire, curling around every part of me. "I just ruined their night," I say, grasping my head with both hands.

Chloe shakes her head. "That was single-handedly accomplished with the strippers." She looks both ways and then grabs my hand. "Come on."

We leave the club, the air of the casino feeling cold on my exposed skin. We don't stop, though, continuing to the exit, where the cold night should be uncomfortable but offers a small amount of comfort as it washes off my regret and embarrassment. Chloe grips my hand tighter, and we walk along the strip, neither of us saying anything. We've hung out numerous times and have talked about academia, football, career goals, and dozens of discussions that have dipped beyond surface topics, but we've never spoken about relationship problems or anything that has cracked the walls we both keep that make us appear like we have our shit together.

She's probably regretting volunteering to walk with me because I have no purpose or idea where I'm going or what I'm doing, and the silence that stretches between us is starting to feel like a physical weight as judgment surpasses shame.

"Come on," Chloe says, giving my hand a gentle tug as she weaves toward the entrance of a hotel. "They have really good burgers here."

Inside, the light of the hotel has me reaching up to wipe at my cheeks again.

"You're okay," Chloe assures me. "You look great."

I stare at her a second, my throat too tight to speak.

"I promise," she says, reading my doubt. She squeezes my hand and leads me farther into the hotel, not stopping until we reach a restaurant. In our short time here, I've learned that people are always hungry, and restaurants always have a waitlist, but by some miracle, they have a small table for us near the back.

"Would you like a drink?" she asks.

I shake my head. "No. I'm pretty sure alcohol fueled that mess." I blow out a long breath, trying to steady my breaths and heart, which both feel erratic and too fast. "God, what did I just do? I ruined everyone's night over something so stupid. That stripper would have moved on in a second if I'd just ignored him."

"You didn't ruin anything. I'm convinced the first night of a Vegas trip is cursed. When Ty, Nessie, Cooper, and I stopped here, I almost punched Tyler in the face." The ghost of a smile tugs at her lips. "Granted, I wanted to punch him in the face a lot that first week of our trip.... But,"—her eyes grow bright, focusing on her point—"I *really* wanted to punch him our first night here in Vegas."

I pull my chin back. I didn't know Chloe before she began dating Tyler, and I barely knew Tyler. They were a packaged deal. "What? I thought you guys were friends for years before you began dating?"

Chloe scoffs and then laughs. "No, definitely not. We avoided and ignored each other."

Shock has my eyes rounding. "Seriously?"

Her smile is genial. "I thought there was no way Ty and I would ever be able to date, if I'm being honest. Not only did I think he was completely arrogant and entitled, but he was also best friends with Coop, and he was a bazillionaire with a plan to move back to England after graduation. It felt like a suicide mission to allow myself to fall for him."

Tears well in my eyes, understanding that feeling so intimately.

"And then, I thought we were over before we really began. We were still in the early honeymoon phase when his dad came and told him he had to return to England. I thought for sure he was gone forever, that he'd find someone else who was prettier, smarter, and wasn't so stubborn and difficult." She purses her lips, then rubs them together. "Sometimes, I still worry that he'll wake up and find someone better."

A tear slips down my cheek.

Chloe passes me a pile of napkins, resting her hand on my forearm.

I shake my head. "There's no way Tyler would ever break up with you." I don't say it as a polite assurance, but as a fact, something more exact than science. "He looks at you like you're the Mona Lisa."

Her eyes dance with a smile. "And most days, I know that, but sometimes insecurities can be really big assholes, and they can feed us lies that feel so damn real, and between school and his work, it can be tough to find time to connect."

More tears fall, the similarities and insecurities between her story and mine so similar. "I feel this on a cellular level."

She nods, lips twisted with a knowing frown. "I know. And I think we need to order some giant burgers with extra cheese, onion rings, and fries, and we need to just bitch about how ridiculous and insane school can be, how terrifying relationships are, how we weren't taught how to adult at all, and how terrible of an idea strippers were, because sometimes we just need to unload."

"I don't know if I can," I tell her, wiping at more tears. "I feel like a leaky faucet at the moment."

"That's okay. You never have to put on a show for me. Tears, anger, sadness, crazy, I'm here for all of it."

"Can we start with the reading assignments?" I ask. "I sometimes feel like they're the academic version of *The Hunger Games*."

She laughs. "It was ridiculous!"

A waitress stops at our table to take our order, and Chloe orders before looking at me for confirmation.

"Two milkshakes," I add.

Chloe grins, nodding, and then we start exchanging stories about school that lead in a myriad of paths, some funny, others disappointing, all of them a shared level of empathy and compassion.

Lincoln

"She's pissed," Pax says, looking toward the door.

"You're great, and your abs are very pretty, but we're good. Thanks," Olivia says, offering one of the strippers her stack of cash.

"This was supposed to be fun. Sexy," Rose says.

Tyler shakes his head, checking his phone for the third time.

"I know, and we appreciate the thought, and we love you for your sexual prowess and confidence, but I don't want to see another guy's package. If I did, I wouldn't be getting married," Olivia tells her.

Their conversation continues, but I drown it out and focus on what to do. My entire life just walked out the door and asked me to wait here, like it's possible for me to breathe in a world without her. This isn't Rae. She doesn't run from things she's afraid of—she runs straight at them. I take a step, but Poppy moves in front of me, staring me down with the same look of warning she reserves for me and anyone who crosses her best friend.

"You won't find anyone better than Rae," she says, stamping her fists to her hips. "And I swear to God if you even consider bringing this other girl around—"

"Other girl?"

She glares at me. "Don't play dumb with me."

"Did you hit your head? I don't know what in the hell you're talking about?"

Poppy narrows her eyes. "You know what you'll lose if you're lying, right?"

"She seriously thinks...?" My thoughts shift to Rae's question about jerseys, the accusation in her stare, and then the stupid exchange in the hallway knocks the wind out of me like a linebacker coming full force down the field. "For fuck's sake, why didn't she say anything?" I rake a hand through my hair.

"She doesn't want to ruin the weekend for everyone."

I shift to take the stairs, but Poppy weaves with me, staring me down like a damn snake charmer.

"I'm not cheating on Rae, for Christ's sake. She's the only one. She always has been, she always will be."

Poppy purses her lips, my response clearly catching her off guard. "But you told her you were at practice, and you weren't."

"Because I was picking up her engagement ring."

"I'm drunk, but I'm not that drunk," she says, shaking her head. "What are you talking about."

"I bought her a ring because she may not know it now, but she's my world, my everything, and she's going to marry me one day."

"You bought her a ring? What about your neighbor? The orange? The cookies? The goddamn jersey?"

"What fucking orange?"

Poppy blindsides me, wrapping her arms around my shoulders and hugging me, her grip shockingly tight. "You have no idea how relieved I am to hear this." She sighs, dropping her arms back to her sides, her expression no longer angry and aggressive but verging on remorseful. "I'm sorry for getting your girlfriend drunk. She needed to get out of her own thoughts tonight. She's got a civil war happening up there between thinking you're moving on, and wanting to quit school, and feeling guilty for telling you no, and not being there for Pax's and mine's engagement...."

"Moving on? Quitting school?" I glance at Paxton as he moves to Poppy's side. "Did she talk to your dad again?" He has a history of making Rae doubt herself and her dreams.

Poppy shakes her head. "I don't think so."

"I need to talk to her. I shouldn't have let her go."

Poppy steps with me, blocking my path once again. "I've always been team Lincoln, even before you deserved it." She smirks. "I didn't think there was a chance you would cheat on her. I mean, I've seen the way you look at her—the way you've *always* looked at her—but jersey girl showing up with cookies and the orange thing, along with you not being at practice like you told Rae, did freak me out a little. But you didn't do anything wrong, neither has she." Poppy gives a gentle shrug.

"But...." I say when she doesn't continue.

"When I thought you were cheating, I wanted to castrate you, but since I know you're not, I want to help you because if there's one thing I'm sure of when it comes to my best friend, it's that you make her happy. In her world, you're the axis. You make her brave and fearless and determined, but with all those empowering strengths, you're also the source of her greatest fears. Sometimes, I think she still doesn't think she deserves you."

I shake my head, taking a step around Poppy, dismissing her rejections that fall on my back.

I turn at the top of the stairs, searching for Paxton. He steps forward, sliding an arm around Poppy's shoulders so she doesn't follow me. "Biggest game of your life right here," he says. "She's fast, stubborn, and damn good at reading the field. Show her your cards." He throws me something that I catch. "All of them." I glance at what he tossed and find a deck of cards. I don't wait for a further explanation before pocketing them and turning for the exit.

Tyler joins me, falling into step as I take the stairs. "They're at a burger joint," he says as we reach the bottom of the stairs.

We make our way through the club and out of the casino, my gait sure, a contradiction to the thoughts running through my head. I question how we got back to this territory of misconceptions and internalized fears and wonder if we ever really left.

"Do you need a ride? A car? How can I help?" Tyler asks.

15

LINCOLN

I shake my head. "I just need to talk to her."

We continue down the Strip, slowing as a group staggers and laughs in front of us. I glance at my watch, reading the late hour and wondering where her thoughts are since it's taking me this long to reach her.

"Chloe won't make things worse. She likes you, and she adores Rae. If it were Nessie, I'd be worried, but Chloe will be trying to help."

I glance at him. "In reverse roles, how would you be feeling?"

Ty shakes his head. "I'd be losing my fucking shite," he admits. "Because that's what love does. It wrings you out, pulls you inside out, and hurts like hell while simultaneously being the most mind-blowing and amazing feeling imaginable."

I grip the spot in my chest where a dull ache has been residing for the past two months and follow Tyler into a casino and down a long hall, stopping at the entrance of a restaurant.

Chloe and Rae sit side by side rather than across from each other —their backs turned to the restaurant.

As we get closer, Rae turns, looking over her shoulder at me, and to my surprise, she looks almost relieved. She leans close to Chloe and says something, who looks over at us as well. Her smile is automatic and grows as she looks past me to Tyler, who pats my shoulder.

Chloe stands, a basket of onion rings in her hand. "Do you think we can take these?"

Tyler's face splits with a grin as he waves her over.

I move closer, sliding onto the bench seat across from Rae.

"I'm sorry for leaving like I did," she says before I can formulate my own apology. "And for making such a scene and leaving you behind to clean it all up."

I shake my head. "There was no scene. When we left, the female strippers were showing the other girls how to do a striptease, and the guys were ordering a round of drinks."

Her shock quickly turns into relief, but unease remains, visible in her squared shoulders and the thoughts racing behind her blue eyes.

I pull out the deck of cards Pax had given me, open the box, and shuffle. Rae watches me, confusion marring her brow. I slide the tray to the opposite side of the table, clearing the space between us. I split the deck, handing her half of the cards. She stares at them and then looks at me.

"What are these?"

"Our truths," I tell her, tossing a card to the table. "There's no other girl. There will *never* be another girl."

Rae stares at me, a contradiction of emotions warring in her gaze. "Poppy told you?"

"Not everything, but I think I've pieced it together." I shake my head. "She's no one. I don't know her. I helped her find her cat while you were gone."

"You gave her a signed jersey."

"It fell out of a box of jerseys I was supposed to sign, and she picked it up before I could get to it. I didn't even realize the correlation to the orange until Poppy pointed it out. It meant nothing to me. She means nothing."

Rae drops a card to the table. "She makes me feel insecure and a little crazy. I'm used to girls falling for you and staring at you, but this felt so personal. I don't know if it's because she's your neighbor, or because it felt so blatant, or because things have been so off with us, but it really shook me." She licks her lips, then sinks her teeth into the bottom one, her face flushed with emotions she's working to abate.

I toss a card on top of hers. "I was ready to kill that stripper tonight. I feel that same brand of jealousy, babe, and I'll be damned if someone tries to tell me that it makes us wrong to feel that way. It's a reaffirmation that we care and don't want to lose each other."

She looks at me, unblinking, then her shoulders fall with relief. Slowly, she drops a card to the table. "I want to quit school."

I consider all the objections I want to tell her but realize my admission might be a better tactic. I cover her card with my own. "The night before the draft, I got wasted and was ready to quit football and work for my dad because I refused to move out of state and away from you."

She shakes her head. "I wouldn't have let you. No way." She shakes her head again.

A smirk claims my mouth. "That's how I feel when hearing you say you want to quit school."

"Getting my doctorate will only be harder and take more time. I barely see you or my family." Tears well in her eyes. "It's only going to get harder."

"Then maybe you take a year off. Maybe you slow down and don't worry about getting it in the shortest window but in a more manageable time frame. And if you decide you still want to quit, then I will support your decision a hundred and ten percent."

Rae stares at me, silently considering the suggestion. Her thoughts visibly shift, and she puts down a card. "I sent Maverick a Christmas present."

The corner of my mouth fights to smile. "I know."

I set down two cards. "I still don't know how I feel about the situation with my dad. I didn't like Carol, but it pisses me off that my dad had an affair and that he kept it a secret for so long. And I sure as hell don't know how to feel about having a younger brother. I'm not about it, and I think if I'm being honest, I was kind of hurt. Hurt that he hadn't told me about him sooner and because I felt like I'd been replaced."

"I'm sorry," she says, sorrow and empathy reflecting in her blue eyes. "That dinner wasn't fair at all. Your dad was unrealistic and selfish, expecting you to take the news lightly. I still regret not having called you and telling you not to come."

I shake my head. "Don't carry that regret. Can you imagine having told me the news later by yourself?"

She winces. "No, but I'm pretty sure it would have had a better outcome, regardless."

I stare at her, waiting to see if she brings up the proposal, wondering if she'll ask me if I regret it or if there was a shred of sincerity in the question.

She knows me well enough. She can likely hear my thoughts because she swallows and plays another card. "I miss college. I miss when we were all together. I miss seeing you and stupid parties and thinking we were busy, and our schedules were crazy when it was a fraction of today's insanity."

I drop a jack. "I don't."

Surprise reflects in her blue gaze as she pulls her chin back a fraction.

"You barely censor yourself around me anymore. And I don't miss the drama or the newness when expectations and unspoken words flooded our interactions. And I don't miss Candace and her drama."

She frowns. "I hadn't thought of that. Or all the drama with my dad."

"Or the accident," I say, my attention cutting to her arm and the scar that serves as a physical reminder of that night. "Or the fucking cranes." I shake my head. "We spent the better part of a year trying to fight our damn feelings for each other. There's no way I want to go back and do that shit again. My patience for Paulson would land me in prison."

"But there were good times, too," she argues. "Look at your senior year."

Memories flash before me, ones of Rae wearing my jersey, my

number painted on her cheek, of her birthday party and the treasure hunt, of taking her to Turks and Caicos for our first big trip over spring break. "Senior year was great, but I still wouldn't go back. I love waking up on my days off and finding you in my T-shirt and your socks. And having couch sex, and kitchen table sex, and shower sex. I love that we have our own space and can do whatever in the hell we want when we want. And more important than any of that is, with the exception of the past few months, we don't dance around shit anymore. We both know where we stand, and that means more to me than anything. My parents failed because they were constantly trying to pacify each other and themselves. I don't want that. These last few months, I've been going out of my head because it feels like we're doing the same shit they did when what we've needed to do was just shed the gloves and have this out."

I drop the remaining cards on the short pile. "We won't ever be able to go back. We're going to continue to grow and change—both of us, and so will everything around us."

She plays a single card. "That scares me."

I shake my head. "Everything changes, but that doesn't have to be a bad thing or mean things don't last. One day, you're going to understand exactly how much I want you—how badly I need you. In this crazy world, you are the only thing—*the only one*—who makes sense to me. You make me a better person, a better everything, but more importantly, you give me purpose and reason and sanity. It's you, Rae. It's always been you. I don't know how or why, but I know I am meant for you, and you're for me. I could tell you I love you a million times, and it wouldn't be enough because love doesn't suffice to describe how I feel for you. What I feel for you is so much bigger than a word. It's the way you make me feel, it's that look you give me like you can't see my flaws or mistakes, it's coming home and seeing your car and knowing you're upstairs, and my sheets smelling of your perfume. It's about forever."

A tear slips from her eye, grazing her cheek before it falls to the table. Rae reaches forward, placing her hand on mine. "I love you so much it terrifies me."

"That fear is like the jealousy," I tell her, brushing my thumb across her knuckles. "It's why I know we'll last because we both know the consequence of losing each other and the significance of that loss."

"Can I amend my answer?"

I stare at her, knowing full well she's referring to the proposal. "No."

She retracts, everything about her pulling back fractionally, but I hold her hand tighter in mine, refusing to allow doubt into her thoughts, and lean closer. "I don't want to tell our kids that story, either. I want the moment that you make the decision to spend the rest of your life with me to be perfect, flawless."

Rae shakes her head. "I don't. I don't want perfect. I want real. I want the jealousy, the anger, the passion, and the moments when we're laughing so hard we can't breathe, and the calm—the real us is perfect." She drops her remaining cards.

I dig my wallet from my back pocket, flipping it open with one hand because I refuse to let go of Rae's. I drop a crisp hundred-dollar bill on the table.

"This isn't a hundred dollars worth of food."

I slide my wallet back into my pocket and stand. "Come on." I give her a playful tug, and her responding laugh makes my chest swell with adoration and love as things slide back into their rightful places.

Rae stands, wrapping her arms around my shoulders, and she steals my entire focus, distracting me from everyone and everything as her mouth collides with mine. Need and relief are like two tides, crashing together as I kiss her, demanding more and giving her everything I have.

Cheers break through the invisible barrier she erected, and Rae shakes her head, kissing me again. "Ignore them." She kisses me again, but I can feel the smile on her lips.

"Hotel," I tell her, walking toward the exit, her still tangled in my arms.

Rae nods, her hands bracketing my cheeks as she kisses me.

I bump into a table, causing a quick reaction of grumbles and then a splash that soaks my right leg with something cold.

"Sorry," I say as Rae straightens and slowly peers around at the onlookers.

I fish my wallet out again and drop another hundred-dollar bill on the table. "I'm really sorry," I tell them. "I wasn't paying attention. Is everyone okay?" I take a quick inventory of the spilled drink and displaced fries and drop another hundred. "I'm sorry."

"Wait. I know you," a guy at the table says.

I flash him a quick smile but cut the conversation short with another apology, my hands falling to Rae's waist and guiding her out of the restaurant.

"Chloe gave me a card," she says, stopping and turning to face me. "She said to call if we need a ride." She reaches into her purse and pulls a small business card and her phone out. I set my hand on her waist, moving my thumb across her hip.

"Hi." Trepidation has her looking nervous. "I'm sorry to bother you, but I was wondering if it would be possible to have a car pick us up from a hotel and bring us back to the Banks Resort?"

Her soft tone and sweet words do something to my chest. Sweet, assertive, stubborn, kind, giving—it's all these pieces of her that remind me how perfect she is, how right she is for me.

Their response makes her smile. She thanks them twice before she hangs up, her smile victorious. "They said someone's already outside."

Tyler. I'm sure he arranged it. I make a mental note to thank him later.

We climb into the back of the car, the energy between us causing me to release the top few buttons of my shirt.

Rae looks at me, her eyes filled with desire as her gaze drops from my mouth to my lap.

Fuck me.

We have to wait for pedestrians on three separate occasions. The final pause makes me consider hopping out of the car, throwing Rae over my shoulder, and sprinting the remaining distance.

Beside me, she laughs quietly, reading my impatience.

"Soak this up because this right here is like going back in time to living with three other dudes."

She tilts her head back and laughs louder, her hand falling to my thigh. "Your pants are soaked."

With what I'm betting is Coke based upon the smell. Totally worth it. I lean close enough that my lips brush her ear. "I'm going to make you twice as wet in about two minutes."

A heavy breath falls from her, and her hand constricts.

When we finally pull up to the hotel, neither of us waits for our door to be opened. I pass the driver a tip and have to jog to catch up with Rae as she steps into the hotel.

"Trying to ditch me?" I tease, wrapping my hand around her hip and pulling her close.

She answers with another smile, this one broader, fuller, reminding me of how much I've missed seeing the expression and how much time we allowed to be taken from us as we lived in our own heads.

"I can read your mind," she reminds me. "These heels slow me down, so I knew I needed a head start, so you didn't throw me over your shoulder and act like a caveman."

"You like when I act like a caveman."

"More than I should," she admits, stopping at the elevators.

The doors slide open, and a half dozen people follow us inside.

"More college flashbacks," I say, inching closer to her, spanning my hand to touch more of her. It hardly soothes my desperation to feel and be close to her.

Slowly, the others get off at multiple floors, leaving us with only two floors until the doors part, and we nearly bolt from the confines. Rae pauses, looking back at me as she opens her purse.

I walk closer, dropping my shoulder and lifting her, so I don't knock the air from her as I pick her up.

She squeals with laughter. "What are you doing?"

"More college flashbacks," I remind her, making my way down the winding hall to our suite.

Raegan

Lincoln hangs the "do not disturb" sign before closing the door behind us, single-handedly since I'm still balanced on one shoulder.

He leaves the lights off, stalking to the bedroom, his steps measured and even, like my weight isn't taxing.

We stop at the edge of the bed, and Lincoln pulls the covers fully back, exposing the white sheets before laying me across the bed. My cheeks ache from a smile that feels like it's never going to fade.

Lincoln strips out of his sports jacket, dropping it to the floor before kicking off his shoes and releasing the cuffs of his shirt. "There's one point we didn't get to," he says, freeing the remaining buttons of his shirt, which he shrugs off. The faint light from the city highlights each hard muscle of his torso and arms, a hypnotic sight that renders me speechless for several seconds.

He gently catches my leg and runs his hands down, slipping my high heel off before doing the same on my opposite foot. His eyes are intent and focused as he skates his hands back up my legs, dragging the skirt of my dress up high on my hips and not stopping until it's pooled around my waist. His touch is soft like a secret, hooking his fingers into the sides of my underwear and slipping them down my legs.

My breaths grow quicker as a heaviness grows between my legs. Every part of me feels impossibly sensitive and desperate for his touch.

Lincoln pushes his wet jeans off, leaving his boxer briefs on before kneeling on the bed. He hovers over me, weight balanced on his fists. "I am yours. Every part of me that you're willing to accept, it's yours. All of me."

His words are a sobering reminder, one that I knew but lost sight of in a mess of assignments, long nights, goals, and a dozen other distractions that, in comparison, are grossly inconsequential.

I reach for him, my arms twining around the back of his neck, pulling our bodies flush, sealing my lips over his. He kisses me back like we have something to prove. I kiss him like I have something to finish. I know my insecurities will likely follow me, as much as I wish I could shed them. They're a part of me like scars, but like those marks, they fade, unlike my feelings for Lincoln, which five years later are stronger and greater than they've ever been.

Lincoln brushes his fingers over me, trailing to the space between my legs, before he gently parts my folds, my entire body aching with need as his touch remains frustratingly gentle. He traces over my most sensitive part, and my legs tremble in response as I suck in a breath, so distracted I can't kiss him back.

He brushes his fingers over me, his movements and pressure increase, and my next exhale is his name as I fist the sheets and lean my head back, losing myself to his touch.

"I'm yours," he says, kissing my chin, and then my cheek, and my jaw. "Only yours." He stands, and I miss the heat and weight of him until he lowers his face between my legs, and his tongue touches my sensitive flesh as he slips a finger inside of me, knowing exactly how and where to touch me. His mouth works me into a frenzy that his fingers work to ease, and then I'm spiraling, calling out his name as an orgasm rips through me, leaving me trembling and so euphoric it feels as though I'm floating.

Lincoln drops his underwear, and I sit up, pulling my dress over my head and tossing it to the end of the bed as Lincoln's strong hands thread behind me and release my strapless bra.

I lie back as he kisses a path up my body, stopping on my breasts for a few moments before he moves to my mouth and kisses me senseless. I forget everything I've missed as I relish in how the years of experience between us has made sex shockingly better as he explores my body like he drew every line and space, knowing exactly where I need and want him because Lincoln Beckett has always possessed and consumed every part of me.

"One more thing," he says, running his thumbs across my nipples, causing my desire to stir and my breath to hitch. "On Wednesday, we're going house shopping." His thumbs and forefingers roll my nipples, the sensation so strong I feel it between my legs. "I want to move in with you. I want it to be our house, our bed, our space."

"Do you know how much I make at the aquarium?"

He stops, his gaze a silent demand for me to listen to him. "I don't care how much you make or don't make. If you didn't love your damn job so much, I'd be campaigning for you to quit and would have years ago because selfishly, I want that time. But, if you think I care about the money, then you don't understand what I'm saying when I tell you that I'm yours. My money is yours, my heart is yours, my life is fucking yours. My soul, everything. It's all yours."

I've never been attracted to Lincoln for his money. The extravagant trips he's taken me on are something I've struggled to accept and get used to, but I think about what it would be like in a reverse role, if I had signed a multi-million-dollar contract. My lasting reservations vanish.

We stare at each other, silent words passing between us of understanding and recognition that has a gentle smile appearing on his face. "Now you're getting it," he says. "My proposal was ill-timed and poorly executed but fully sincere. I want to spend the rest of my days with you, and I want it to start now. One closet, one bed, one house."

Tears blur his expression. "I love that idea," I whisper, my voice wavering. "I love you, every part of you, I want and need. And I am just as fully yours."

Lincoln dips his head, brushing his lips against mine. "That's all I need." He kisses me again, and then he buries himself inside me, pleasure racing through me as I whisper his name.

He growls in response. His thrusts are controlled and measured, creating waves of pleasure that have my body moving and responding like I'm a marionette. His movements become faster and deeper, his breaths still shockingly even when my own are rasps and gulps as blood whooshes in my ears, and my thighs begin to tremble. Then I'm lost, riding the high of my second orgasm that Lincoln chases, his hands gripping my waist as he pumps into me, finding his own release.

16

RAEGAN

I wake up, and for the first time in months, it's next to Lincoln. His body is warm, pressed up against my back, one arm securely around my waist.

I lie still, appreciating the moment, absorbing every detail. I consider his suggestion about slowing down with school or taking a leave from the aquarium for a short while. Neither option is overly appealing because I've always been one who takes too much on, a habit I likely learned from both of my parents who struggled to have enough time and money while I was growing up, so they raced to get it done as fast as possible so they could land a new job or promotion in hopes of making more money. It's the definition of a rat race, wrapped in the pursuit of making the best life for my siblings and me. I was lucky and had Grandpa, so I wasn't left unattended for great lengths of time, but without him, it likely would have been a lonely childhood, and I've often wondered if them both chasing the next goal was the demise to my parent's relationship.

I carefully shift to move as little as possible to grab my phone from the nightstand. It's just past ten, and already I have half a dozen messages, most of them dating back to last night.

Poppy: Lincoln's on his way, and I think you should talk to him. Jersey girl was a Candace. #TeamLincoln

Poppy: I love you. Let me know if you need ANYTHING.

Chloe: There's a car outside for you guys. We love you and hope everything goes smoothly. If you need space, there will be a hotel room with your name on it.

Arlo: Rae Rae, Liv and I love you!!!

Poppy: I need an update.

I grin and start with a reply to Poppy.

Me: I'm still Team Lincoln, too.

Poppy: He was legit scared last night. He really loves you.

Me: I know, and I legit love him.

Lincoln presses a kiss to my bare shoulder and then stretches, each hard plane of muscle constricting.

"I'm team Raegan," he says, his voice gravelly from sleep.

"I wasn't trying to wake you."

He brushes his lips over my shoulder again. "I slept like a rock."

"Good sex can do that." I shift, moving so I can face him. His dark hair is deliciously disheveled, and his brown eyes shine with humor and warmth.

He chuckles. "Good sex and having you beside me." He pulls me closer. "I do miss this about college. Now, it always feels like I'm sneaking out of bed, and you're sneaking into bed."

I trace invisible patterns across his chest with my fingers, absorbing the feel of his warm skin. "Me too."

"We should make a list for the realtor. Pax said it helped narrow down the searches."

I drop a kiss on his shoulder and prop myself up with one arm, a hand against my cheek. "I don't want you to feel like we have to move because your neighbor made me insecure. I was thinking about it this morning and realized how silly and insignificant this problem is. I mean, we've washed our hands of it. You don't need to move. I even helped pick out the condo."

He reaches forward, brushing some stray hairs behind my ear. "Maybe we'll keep it, too. But we're going to need a guesthouse so everyone can come to visit us."

"Guesthouse?" I ask. "You mean a guest room."

He grins. "Did I mention how much I love our fucking privacy?"

Laughter bubbles out of me. "I didn't realize it was this extreme."

Lincoln nods. "I like the condo, and it's great for when we want to be downtown, but we're going to need more space soon." He rolls, knocking me onto my back and hovering over me. "A bigger shower that we can both fit in." He kisses my lips. "A dining room table to fit both of our dysfunctional families at and Friendsgiving dinners." He kisses my collarbone. "A yard where you can put all two million pumpkins you buy every fall." I laugh as he kisses me between my breasts and scoots lower. "Maybe a nursery one day?" He kisses my stomach, this time lingering there, his lips and hands so impossibly tender.

Images of Lincoln being a dad, this impossibly strong man holding a tiny baby, grow into imagining him helping a teetering baby with their first steps, to running. Sleeping bags and flashlights in the living room when Seattle insists on raining out a campout. Goosebumps descend over my skin, knowing how protective and loving Lincoln will be, how perfect he's going to be in the role of dad.

"And your home office where you'll be finding ways to save the planet." He kisses my stomach again, and for a hot minute, I want to announce I'm quitting school and life and that he's filing for early retirement, and we're going to stay here in this room in this bed forever and have a dozen babies.

"Can we balance it all?"

Lincoln lifts his face to look at me and slowly moves back up my body. "Absolutely. We make the rules, babe. You and me." His stare is a promise, an oath that I sign by kissing him. He groans in response, a deep and husky sound that builds a promise between my legs.

My phone vibrates, and then so does his. A chorus of sounds that has Lincoln swearing as he swipes for his phone. I reach for mine as well.

Poppy: Get dressed. We're going to breakfast because we're all team buffet ;)

Lincoln tries to look grumpy, but humor is bright in his eyes. "Even sleeping in the same building is impossible with these clowns." He looks at me again, an expression so loving and affectionate that it makes me want to bask under his gaze all day, feeling the warmth of his skin, trust, and support.

WE TEST the size of the hotel shower, trying three different sex positions to determine what size of a shower we want in our new home, and Lincoln delivers a shattering orgasm that makes my legs feel like jelly.

"We'll definitely need a bench," he says, wrapping a plush towel around my shoulders.

"I'd never leave."

His smile is wolfish. "That's the idea."

On our ride down to the lobby, my nerves begin a direct course to my brain, reminding me of last night and how I'd left mid-striptease. "What am I going to say?" I ask, turning to Lincoln.

He shakes his head. "They're not mad or upset. They just want to make sure everything's okay."

"Rae Rae!" Arlo calls my name as the elevator doors open.

Lincoln keeps his gaze pinned on me. "I'm right beside you."

I weave my fingers with his, and we step off the elevator, discovering the others are all gathered by one of the fountains, waiting for us.

"I'm so sorry for last night," I start.

Olivia shakes her head. "There's no need to apologize. We've all had our moments, and we'll continue to have them, and we'll be here for each other through the thick and the thin. That's what best friends are for."

Poppy grins. "Ride or die for life."

EPILOGUE
LINCOLN

Christmas the following year

"Maybe we should get a couple more wreaths?" Rae turns to look at me.

I swallow my objections and stare at the house we moved into three months ago, just in time to fill the porch with pumpkins and straw bales. It's an old Victorian house tucked farther away from Seattle than we'd planned. When we first came to see it, the Japanese maples that lined the driveway were starting to turn colors, and then we saw a half dozen squirrels and three deer walk into the yard, and because I'm fairly sure Rae is a direct descendant of Snow White, they didn't run when she got out of the car. Instead, they looked at her with curiosity and patience, and Rae was ready to move in without even seeing the house. It's not our final house, which will be oceanfront, a place where Rae can peer out at the waves and remember her love for the ocean and the animals, but for now, this place feels like home.

"Where are we going to put more wreaths?" I ask.

Raegan grins. This smile could get me to agree to any damn thing she suggests, including a hundred more wreaths if that's what she wants. "That was an impressively controlled 'hell no.'"

I wrap my free hand around her hip, drawing her as close as her puffy coat allows, and kiss her temple, staring at our house lined with clear Christmas lights, a wreath hung by red ribbons on every window and door. "I'm just concerned that if we hang another wreath, the whole front of the house might fall over because we've essentially hung the weight of three trees across it."

She giggles in response, folding our hands together. "Come on. I'm eating my celebratory Christmas vacation cheesecake in bed."

"In bed?" I ask, walking up the front steps with her.

"Clothing optional. It's invite-only, so you might want to behave."

"Tell me how many more wreaths you want, and they'll be here by morning."

Her smile is so broad and genuine it steals my breath. These are the moments—these tiny fractions of time when we find joy and laughter in simplicity and details—that confirms what I've known since meeting her that we belong together. "I was referring to the raccoon you were trying to shoo before we left."

"I'm sure Coach will be completely understanding of me needing time off for rabies."

Her laughter explodes as she grabs a small package off the porch while I open the front door.

Inside, I hit the switch that connects to the Christmas tree in our living room. This year, we didn't hold back or delay getting the house ready for Christmas, something I still regret from last year. And I'm damn glad because every time Raegan walks past one of the two trees we set up, she smiles. Garlands snake around every window, glowing warmly with lights and red ribbons, and the fireplace has stockings hung with block letters that read "MERRY."

Nerves thrum in my chest, an energy that's been following me for most of the past year distracting me as Rae opens the box.

"Oh, it came! Check this out, babe." Rae holds up a tiny blue and green baby outfit with Lawson written across the back.

"Pax is going to love that," I tell her.

Her eyes are bright and knowing. "I haven't gotten either of them a single gift meant for them, everything's for the baby, and he's not even born yet."

It's a close competition to see who's most excited for Poppy and Paxton's firstborn. Paxton has been walking around like a god, and Rae and Poppy text daily with Poppy's pregnancy updates, and their Grandpa Cole and Camilla, and Rae's mom are all ready for the next generation of Lawson children. "I don't think they'll mind."

Rae nods, breaking down the box that she goes to put in the recycle bin in the garage before coming back to the entryway. "How's your shoulder feeling?" Rae asks, putting her shoes away in the front closet.

"Great," I tell her, leaning on the doorjamb and helping her out of her coat.

She eyes me suspiciously. My shoulder injury from my sophomore year at Brighton still flares up, and after our game last week against the Broncos, where I had been clipped, I spent the following two days with ice packs strapped to me.

"We should put some ice on it."

I shake my head. "It's movie time." I toe off my shoes and set them beside hers. It's a simple detail, our things next to each other, but one that makes me smile every damn day. I miss certain aspects of the condo, the convenience to restaurants and shows, the views of the city, the quick commute to the practice facility—but out here, the space, the quiet, the fact that everything of Rae's sits beside everything of mine more than makes up for those minor losses.

"Tell me it's a Christmas movie, and I'll lose my pants here and now," she says.

"We might have to play a double feature."

Her shoulders sag, making me laugh. I lift the bag with our cheesecakes that we'd ordered to go. "I have your consolation prize."

She flashes that smile, the same one that hits me squarely in the heart and blinds me to the rest of the world. "I'll grab the forks," she says.

The silverware clinks as she opens the drawer. "Remind me, what time is your dad coming by tomorrow?"

"He hasn't confirmed," I tell her.

Rae appears with two forks. "But he's bringing Maverick?"

I nod. Over the past year, my dad and I have been working toward finding a new normal again. My relationship with Maverick will never be similar to the one Rae shares with her siblings. We'll never go to parties or college together. We won't have a childhood of memories constructed of holidays and family vacations and bouts of the flu, like the Lawsons share. However, I've realized I'd still punch someone in the face for Maverick—and when he experiences his first heartbreak, I'll be there with solid advice and a shoulder. Perhaps fate had a hand in teaching me what siblings are supposed to look like and gave me some of the best role models prior to me having a sibling of my own. "I'm guessing they'll be here around five," I say as she stands beside me, her cold hand curling around mine.

I lead her upstairs to the master bedroom, my favorite room in the house. It's huge, arguably too big. Our bed sits against one wall, and a giant TV is across from it, perfect for movie nights.

"I'm putting on sweats first," she says, releasing my hand and entering our closet, which connects to the master bathroom.

She's out of sight for a second when she gasps, and the lights flip on.

My adrenaline spikes as I move forward, but then she starts laughing.

"I can't get used to this closet," she says as I round the corner. Her cheeks are the same shade of pink as when she's nervous or embarrassed as she points at the giant mirror that hangs against the wall. "My reflection startles me daily." She shakes her head. "Pax would go to town if he knew this."

Truthfully, I've been caught off guard by it a time or two myself. "Maybe we should have some low light motion detector lights installed in here?"

"Or take down the mirror." She folds the jeans she'd been wearing, returning them to a compartment on her side of the closet.

"We could bring it out to the bedroom," I suggest. "Place it where I can always see both sides of you."

Rae pulls on a pair of black and white checkered pants. "You like my sweatpants that much?" She strikes a pose.

Innuendos and promises of what I love about her body that involve this mirror are stacking in my head like a tower of Jenga, ready to collapse and change the trajectory of this night. "I meant while I'm buried inside of you," I tell her. "That's the point of a sex mirror. Ask Chloe."

Rae shakes her head. "I still think Tyler and Chloe's mirror is a dressing mirror."

In April, we traveled to England and saw Tyler, Chloe, Nessie, and Cooper for an entire week. When Chloe had given us a tour of their house, Raegan commented on how pretty the sizable ornate mirror in their bedroom was, which has since led to a dozen conversations about the mirror's purpose.

I shake my head. "It's a sex mirror."

"How do you know?"

"Because it's in their bedroom."

"People get dressed in their bedrooms."

"Babe, that mirror has one sole purpose, and that's to watch each other while they fuck. They might check to make sure their clothes are on straight afterward, but that's not its primary purpose."

Rae stares at me, lips pursed with a question or thought. I'm expecting her to remind me that not everyone has such dirty thoughts as I do. "Maybe we should move it tomorrow. I have an entire week off to try it out."

Thoughts of watching Raegan in the mirror while sliding in and out of her, watching each expression as I bend her over the bed, the sight of her back arching as she rides me, they nearly undo me and have me testing my strength to move the mirror here and now all by myself when in reality it probably needs two or three of us—definitely none of them being Paxton.

The idea of my best friend is as unwelcomed as it is appreciative as my tower of thoughts continues to sway and tilt. "We won't be leaving this house for the next week." I'm considering who to call tomorrow to help me move it as I take a few steps back to gain some necessary distance. "I'm going to get the cheesecake ready," I tell her, heading back out to the bedroom. I pat my pocket for the millionth time and discreetly remove a wire from the back of the TV.

"For the record, I had a mirror in my bedroom at my parents' house, and it was strictly for getting dressed," Rae says.

I grin. "Get your head out of the gutter, Lawson."

She scowls at me, an expected reaction whenever I use her last name.

I grab the remote and pretend to turn it on. "Shit. It's not working," I say.

"Maybe it's the batteries," Rae suggests.

"Why don't we go watch the movie in the family room."

She looks from me to the bed, indecision and reluctance visible as she pulls in a breath and holds it.

"Come on. I'll rub your feet, and we won't get crumbs in the bed. It will be a win-win."

"You're right, it's not a big deal. But we should figure out why the TV's not working. It was working this morning."

"Tomorrow," I tell her, grabbing our dessert.

"Let me just grab socks."

I nod, already halfway to the door. "I'll meet you in the loft."

My heart is in my throat. It feels like I'm going to throw it up at any second as I make my way to the large room that was meant to be a bonus room that we've converted into a space to watch football and movies. When Rae isn't buried with school, she'll help me digest tape. Tonight, it hardly reflects its usual purpose.

Tonight, the room has strands of clear Christmas lights hanging across the ceiling and walls, spaced by the strings that have hundreds of photos hanging from them of Rae and me together. They're suspended by tiny clips that I continuously broke until Poppy fired me from the task. The pictures span from our earliest days, before we were officially a couple, to just last weekend.

Red rose petals are scattered across the floor, with battery-lit candles filling the space.

I blow out a long breath, hearing Rae's footsteps. I turn as she stops in the doorway. She looks at me like a deer caught in the headlights, then peers around at the flower petals, the bouquets that line every surface, the thousand candles that we went overboard on. Finally, she returns her eyes to me, and she takes a step into the room, then another. With each move closer to me, my heart stutters, but my nerves calm. It's a contradiction that makes me feel lightheaded and nauseous and somehow completely grounded.

"Hey, Kerosene," I say, reaching a hand toward her. "I have something for you to watch."

She steps closer, placing her hand in mine before she leans forward to look more closely at the strings of photos. "Oh my gosh. That's us from the park clean-up. And my birthday scavenger hunt." She looks at me, adoration and nerves reflecting back at me, likely matching my expression.

"I have a theme," I tell her, hitting "play" on the remote.

Across the TV, it reads, "Raegan, have I told you how long I've loved you?" It cuts to a video of me, my senior year of college. Arlo is by my side, recording us as we celebrate Ian's birthday. "Tell me again why it doesn't matter if you're drafted," Arlo prompted.

I shrugged. "Because I'm going to marry Rae, and that's all that matters."

Rae turns, looking at me, but the video continues to one of me that I took of myself when this idea first took shape last year while we were in Vegas.

"I almost proposed to you about a hundred times yesterday, and I'm betting I'll want to propose a thousand more times before I actually do because I've already considered proposing to you a few million times. But I want to do it right this next time and make sure you know you're never a consolation prize or anything less than my number one priority and the person I love most in the world. So, here starts the record. Let's see where it takes us."

Rae looks at me again. "What?" her question is rhetorical, but her shock is genuine.

In the next video, I'm alone in my truck. "We saw fifty gazillion houses today, and I was reminded of one of the million reasons you make me a better person when our realtor kept showing us shit we didn't ask for, and you were so polite and kind and professional about it all while I was ready to walk out." I nodded. "We might live in one of these houses soon.... Well, none of the houses we saw today, but another one, and I am so damn excited."

The video cuts to me on a plane, sitting beside Pax. "Is this one of your videos?" Pax asks.

I nod and hold up a sign that says. "I'm going to marry you one day."

Pax peers at it the paper and grins, then nods at the camera. "I fully support this message ... as long as you sleep in separate beds, in separate rooms."

Then, we're in England. We'd gone South and stayed the night before heading back to see Chloe and Ty. "I'm heading to find some coffee, and I want to tell you, Rae, I almost proposed to you last night, but someone pulled the chain in the hotel bathroom, and the fire alarm went off." I shake my head. "This is me proclaiming my love for you in England." The video cuts to a month later. I'm wearing a pair of sweats, sitting in the locker room. "We just lost a game we shouldn't have, and I'm sitting here realizing I get to go home and see you, and regardless of my joke of a game, you're going to lie and tell me I did great because you love me even when I play like a fucking horse with one leg, and so I'm going to pick up dinner for you now, because I know you've forgotten to eat, and you probably jumped into the ocean again to save another animal, and I'm going to lie and tell you I'm okay with that, because I'm so damn proud of you." The video zooms in way too close. "It still scares the shit out of me every damn time you go into the ocean." It zooms back out. "Can we add that you can't jump into the ocean in our vows?"

The video plays for a solid ten minutes. Some of the clips are as short as a few seconds. Others include her family. Some are of our friends, all of whom learned about my videos and asked to partake in them. Rae laughs at some and wipes her eyes during others.

When the video stops, I drop to one knee, looking at the love of my life as I do. Her hands are shaking as she starts to sink down with me. I shake my head. "You're supposed to be standing," I whisper.

She nods and slowly gets back to her feet, our hands linking without thought or direction.

My nerves stop as I look into her eyes, everything seeming so simple and right in this moment. I smile at her, and her blue eyes radiate warmth and love. "Raegan Eileen Lawson, there isn't a sight I want to see, an experience I want to have, or a single thing I want to do without you by my side. You give me purpose and strength. You are constantly challenging me, fulfilling me, and pushing me. You are the best parts of me, the best parts of my life. And I promise to spend my life loving you, cherishing you, and supporting you, being the partner that you deserve, through thick and thin, always and forever. Will you do me the tremendous honor of—"

"Yes, she says, nodding as she wipes away tears. "Yes. Yes. A million times yes."

I grin. "Of being my wife?" I finish.

She laughs, nodding again. "Absolutely."

For years, I've known that we were meant to be together, that our stories would always include each other, but at this moment, one I will never forget as long as I live, the future and what is to come for us has never been sweeter.

ALSO BY MARIAH DIETZ

The Dating Playbook Series

Bending the Rules

Breaking the Rules

Defining the Rules

Exploring the Rules

Forgetting the Rules

Writing the Rules

The Weight of Rain Duet

The Weight of Rain

The Effects of Falling

The Haven Point Series

Curveball

Exception

Standalones

The Fallback

Tangled in Tinsel, A Christmas Novella

ACKNOWLEDGMENTS

I truly hope you enjoyed returning to the Brighton crew!! This book made my heart so happy, and I absolutely loved that Rae and Lincoln got to make their big gestures and declarations. My heart really needed this story, and I hope it gave you peace as well.

A very special thank you to Ngozi Ejiofor Oguguah, Juliana Martinhão Ignácio, Megan Cox, and Sarah Foster, who allowed me to pick their brains and shared their infinite wisdom with me.

A huge thank you to Lizzy Ganske for being so supportive, patient, and amazing. Your feedback and editing was so crucial to this story.

And Arielle Brubaker for all of your hilarious comments and your endless support as both a friend and editor.

Kate Farlow, you are AMAZING! Thank you for making this epic cover with no time, little direction, and a ton of requests.

And a heartfelt thank you to everyone who takes the time to read this story. Thank you for your support and love. It truly means the world to me.

ABOUT THE AUTHOR

Mariah Dietz is a USA Today Bestselling Author and self proclaimed nerd. She lives with her husband and sons in North Carolina.

Mariah grew up in a tiny town outside of Portland, Oregon where she spent most of her time immersed in the pages of books that she both read and created.

She has a love for all things that include her family, good coffee, books, traveling, and dark chocolate. She's also been known to laugh at her own jokes.

www.mariahdietz.com
mariah@mariahdietz.com
Subscribe to her newsletter, here

Made in the USA
Monee, IL
05 August 2022

11034865R00090